MARKING THE DAYS

NICHOLAS JAGO

DEDICATION

I dedicate this book to, Vincent (Vinny).

He told me to write while he was alive,

but I kept putting it off.

I hope he would have approved and been

proud of me for writing it.

CONTENTS

NOTE TO MY READERS

While this is a work of fiction, please remember there have

been many such crimes in the United Kingdom.

ACKNOWLEDGMENTS

I wish to thank Anthony Duncan for editing my work. Patricia Duncan for formatting and for the cover art-work as well as her encouragement. Pauline Andreani, a French author, friend and brother for inspiring me to put pen to paper. My friends and colleagues in our lock down writers group. My neighbours and friends who have listened patiently and given comments on the work and last, but not least, my family for all their support.

CHAPTER ONE

THE BEGINNING

The town of Newpark is centered around a country park, and about fifteen miles from Peterborough. There is a small shopping mall with restaurants that will serve alcohol only with a meal, a cinema and a variety of shops to suit most tastes, a general store for groceries, and a post office. There is a local garage for fuel and car repairs, a doctor's practice, a dentist, a veterinarian practice, and a primary school. Buses arrive daily to take the older children to the high school that is some ten miles away, on the other side of the county park. There is also a regular bus route with a schedule which allows buses every hour after six-thirty am, and the last bus is at eleven pm.

The houses are no more than two stories high, laid out in neat rows from the central mall and the edge of the park. There are no high-rise or multi-occupied buildings, but the houses vary in size from the smallest two-bedroom houses to the largest, with five bedrooms. Each house has a garden to the rear, of varying sizes, and some of the larger houses are gated, with driveways and splendid front gardens. One main road leads to the centre of the town, and smaller roads twist around the houses with pedestrian lanes and access paths avoiding the main road. There is minimal or 'eco' street lighting, which comes on at dusk and goes off at sunrise. There is a police station and a local bobby who lives in the town with his family, and he knows a few of the residents, and most of those that cause trouble. It is generally a peaceful town with little to no major incidents. The fire department has a small fire station which is staffed by retained fire officers who practise every Thursday night, but who are also ready at a moment's notice to fulfil their obligations. There is a plumber, a car mechanic, a florist and a shopkeeper amongst them, and they will drop whatever they are doing to attend to their duties as fire officers, if their bleeper goes off.

Interestingly, there are no public houses, bars or nightclubs in the town, but there is a gym, a swimming pool and a recreation centre, where many sports are played, including tennis, netball, basketball, five-a-side football and other indoor and outdoor sports.

Many residents work in the town's shops or in the hospitality industry. The local plumber and car mechanic live in modest two-bedroom houses, while the florist and shopkeepers live in the larger three-bedroom houses. The doctor, dentist and veterinarian all drive into the town daily, from their homes in neighbouring villages and towns. Some of the residents travel to Peterborough each day for work, but return in the evening to relax and spend time with their family. The nearest railway station is approximately eight miles away, but the bus service travels and stops at the station. There is also a large car park at the station, so some of the residents drive to the station and travel into Peterborough by the regular train service.

As you can imagine, it is a friendly, dull, and unexciting place to live. But what could be a problem with living in such a safe environment? Well, the problem is mainly with the young people, who need excitement, adventure, and challenges. So, what do they do? All the annoying things that young people can and will do!Riding bikes on the bridleways through the country park and the footpaths, or on the footpaths in the town. Playing music too loud, shouting and screaming at each other, running around in the shopping mall, instead of walking like civilized adults! In other words, they act like most young people! But the majority of them are good kids.

So it was quite a shock to everyone when the body of a young girl was found near the edge of the county park on July the twenty-seventh, at around four pm. Though this did not come to light until the following morning, when the news broke.

Thomas Cooper had been walking his dog, as was his usual practice, when he came across the near-naked female body. His collie dog had been rummaging around in some leaves, and her body had been exposed. He called his dog back and immediately called the police from his mobile phone. He didn't have to get any closer to the body, for he guessed from the pale colour of her skin that she was dead. He didn't wish to get any closer, so he stood a few feet away, put the lead back on his dog, and waited for the police to arrive.

The first on the scene was PC 271 Johnson. He wasn't the local bobby, but had been dispatched from the station when the call came in. He carefully examined the scene without touching or getting too close himself, decided not to interfere with the evidence, and immediately called headquarters for the medical examiner, scene of crime officers (SOCO), and the detectives to attend. They arrived within thirty minutes. PC Johnson took a statement from Thomas Cooper, told him to go home, and asked him not to talk about this to anyone, telling him that very soon he may be subject to further interview. When the detectives arrived, they cordoned off the area with yellow tape. They were careful in examining the body where it lay, and the Scene of Crime Officers, SOCO, or the forensic 'guys', took photographs and recorded all evidence that was necessary in these circumstances, which included footprints, measurements, soil samples etc. One shoe was found close to her body, but the other shoe was missing. Her body was taken to the mortuary where further examination would take place. The preliminary findings by the Medical Examiner, were that from the marks on her neck, she had been strangled. She was possibly sexually assaulted, as she had no underwear on, and there was bruising and some dried blood around her groin area. At this stage, they did not know who she was, and could not definitely say how she died, but it was probably about two hours earlier, as rigor mortis was only just setting in. Several other police officers had arrived, and had set about searching the area for her missing items of clothing, including her shoe.

By seven pm, Mrs. Archer had started to worry about her teenage daughter Sofia. High school had finished a few weeks earlier, and she had told her mother that she was going to enjoy the holidays by spending more time with her friends. She had got up quite early, had breakfast, and left home at around ten am that morning. She had taken a few pounds in her purse to get a coffee or snack during the day. She should have been home by five pm for her tea, but her mother hadn't worried, thinking that she would probably be home by five thirty or six. By seven pm she was worried, and started to telephone her friends. First, she called Cindy Gardener, who had been one of her best friends, but Cindy said she hadn't seen her all day. Then she called Juliette Palmer, who said that she had met her in the morning, and they had gone to the mall. Sofia had said she had to go and meet someone, and left her at about eleven thirty. She didn't know who she was going to meet. Mrs. Archer spoke to her husband, and they decided to call the police.

PC Johnson was sent to interview them, and obtained a photograph of Sofia. He left after taking details of Sofia's friends, and said he would keep in touch, and they should stay home in case she arrived back. Unfortunately, the photograph was that of the dead girl! He didn't tell the family, but reported to the detectives, who by now had set up a mobile unit close to the scene. It was now in their hands.

The post-mortem discovered that the hyoid bone in her neck was broken, and this indicated strangulation.

There was bruising around her wrists and face and skin under her nails. She had internal injuries comparable with sexual intercourse, bruising and blood around the thighs, groin and her vulva was badly torn. There was tearing of the flesh and semen in her vaginal cavity. She had put up a struggle. The skin on the heel of her left foot was torn, indicating that she may have been dragged for some distance. Samples from under her nails and semen were taken and sent off to the lab for DNA analysis. As was found at the scene, her underwear was missing, and her dress was badly ripped. She had no socks or tights on, and only one shoe was found. The police at the scene of the crime searched the area for her missing clothing and purse, but found nothing. Had the murderer taken them for a trophy?

Once it was established and confirmed that it was the body of seventeen-year-old Sofia Archer, the detectives and WPC Scott went to the Archer household to deliver the news to her parents, and ask them to officially identify the body of their daughter. Neither detective liked this part of their job, but they carried it out with compassion and empathy. Now, of course, they had to ask the parents the same questions about their daughter's movements, her friends, and her habits. Did she have a boyfriend, where did she usually go, was she in the habit of using alcohol or drugs? Though nothing was found in her blood, it was essential that they asked, in case it had any relevance to the case. The detectives drove Mr. and Mrs. Archer to the mortuary, where they identified the body of their daughter. Then they were driven back to their home.

Mrs. Archer confirmed the story she had told PC

Johnson and gave the detectives the names, addresses and telephone numbers of the friends she knew Sofia had. She didn't think Sofia used any drugs and she said she was too young to drink alcohol. WPC Scott was left with the family overnight and a PC was left outside to ensure the family's privacy while investigations and interviews took place. By now it was past midnight.

The detective in charge of the investigation was Inspector Simon Amery, who had some twenty years under his belt. He was assisted by Detective Sergeant Keith Merriweather, known as 'Merry' to his colleagues. He'd been in the job for almost fifteen years and had dealt with many murder investigations.

Amery told Merry to go home for the night, as it was too late to interview anyone now, but to be back at six am and they would start the investigation. Merry drove off.

Amery stayed in the mobile unit and started to examine the evidence, and information already obtained, and to decide on a way forward for the investigation.

CHAPTER TWO

DAY TWO

When Merriweather arrived back the following morning, two coffees in hand, Amery was sitting at his temporary desk. Merriweather handed him one of the coffees and said,

"OK, guv, how are we going to handle this today?"

"Right, Merry, first we'll get Johnson to round up some of the kids that Sofia knew, except Juliette Palmer, and we can interview them and ascertain their whereabouts yesterday. Johnson can take them to the police station, and they can wait. You and I will go to see this Juliette Palmer. So Johnson informs me, as far as we knew at the present time, she was the last person to see Sofia. Johnson got me her address, but we need to go now before she leaves home."

"I have spoken to Johnson, and he is already on

the case getting these kids together, and has called the Palmer household, and told them we are on our way. I have got a civilian secretary from the pool to come and assist here, and there will be a police presence outside for security. WPC Scott can stay with the family for the time being, but I'll give her a call after we've been to the Palmer residence, to see if she wants relief, or if she feels she can leave the family."

While Amery and Merriweather drove to the Palmer household, the news of the murder was spreading. The national newspaper, arriving on doorstops and in the local shops, had little information on the incident, describing it as a "MURDER IN A SLEEPY TOWN".

They arrived at the Palmer house at around seven am. It was impressive, with a gated entrance to the drive and an electronic communicator which was used to open the gates, after Amery had introduced himself. Merriweather drove up the gravel path to the house.

Standing at the door was a tall dark-haired young man, about nineteen or twenty years of age. He was dressed in a pair of dark grey trousers and a blue shirt, with a loose grey jumper over the top, and wore a pair of what looked like brand new Gucci trainers. As the two detectives got out of the car and approached the house, the young man called to them.

"Please come in. PC Johnson telephoned to say you were coming to see us, and my parents and sister are in the drawing room, and waiting for you."

He stood erect, motioned with his hand, and

spoke very confidently He took them to the drawing room and introduced his parents, who were both seated on an extremely large settee, and his sister, who was sitting at a table. He was about to leave the room when Amery asked him to stay and, after closing the door, he sat next to his sister at the table.

After introducing himself and Merriweather, Amery started speaking, while Merriweather took out his pocketbook and began making copious notes. This he did throughout the interview.

"I am sure by now you have heard the news, and I need to establish the whereabouts of people." He looked at Juliette and the young man. Juliette would not make eye contact with him.

"I understand that you" - he continued talking to Juliette - "might have been the last person to see Sofia." Juliette looked at him. Amery continued "Can you tell me when you last saw her?"

Juliette, softly spoken and almost whispering, replied,

"It was about eleven thirty, yesterday. Her mum telephoned me last night, and I told her that Sofia and I were at the Mall for a while, just window-shopping or talking to our friends, then having a coke, but Sofia said she had to leave and that was at about eleven thirty."

"I see." replied Amery. "Now just go back a bit for me, will you Juliette? What time did you meet Sofia?"

"It was just after ten am."

"And where did you meet?" he asked.

"We met up at the garage, because she said she wanted to walk with me to the Mall."

"And why do you think she said that?" he questioned her.

"She said she was going to meet someone later, but didn't say who. She wanted us to be together when we went into the Mall."

"Did that seem strange to you?"

"Well, no, not really. Sofia and I live in different parts of town, so meeting at the garage seemed the most central place, and then we wouldn't miss each other in the Mall."

"So, you don't drive?" said Amery.

"No." she replied.

"And after she left you at?" - he paused .

"You said about eleven thirty, so what did you do?"

"I spoke to Stanley, Brian and Ronny, then I did some more window-shopping, bought a little bag, met Cindy, and we went for a coffee and just hung about till about four thirty, then I came home here, and I guess Cindy went home too."

"And you?" Amery turned his attention to the young man. "What is your name?"

"I'm Jonathan."

At this point Mr. Palmer interrupted, "Erm, Inspector, what has my son got to do with this?"

"I am endeavouring to ascertain the whereabouts of everyone at this point, Mr. Palmer, and I will be interviewing a lot of people. I might ask for your whereabouts yesterday?" He put the question to him.

"Well, I really don't understand, but as it happens, I was here all day and so was my wife. We spent the morning in the garden then," His wife interrupted him,

"I did go and fill up the Range Rover about eleven."

"Oh, yes," continued Palmer "but after lunch she" - he pointed to his wife - "went back and pottered around in the garden again, I think, and I watched the TV. It must have been about three thirty when Jonathan came back, and shouted to his mother. I must have dozed off, because that was what woke me, then Juliette arrived home about five pm. We all ate together at six thirty, and it was about seven-ish when Sofia's mother telephoned to speak to Juliette."

Mrs. Palmer nodded and said, "Yes, that's about right. It was such a lovely day. I stayed in the garden until well after four pm, then I came in, had a shower and made dinner, which we all had together at about six thirty."

"Jonathan," said Amery, turning his attention to the young man, who was sitting upright in the chair at the table, not quite as confident as he had appeared to be earlier "tell me, where did you go yesterday?"

"Me?"

"Yes." replied Amery.

"Erm, well," - he coughed a little then continued - "I spent the day at the gym. Went first this morning, and then went for a swim. I left there about three pm and drove home. I got back about three thirty, as Dad said."

"Did you go to the Mall?" asked Amery.

"No!" he answered abruptly.

"Did you see Sofia at all yesterday?"

"No." He answered a bit too quickly for Amery's liking, but Amery didn't press the point.

"How well did you know Sofia?" Amery asked him.

"She was my sister's friend, so I knew her. She had been to the house and I used to see her when I was at school, but I started university last year, so I have only seen her a couple of times since."

"And when do you think the last time you saw her was?"

Jonathan huffed and sighed, and appearing to be thinking about the question, answered "Last time she stayed over here."

"Which was when?" Amery questioned.

"About a week ago."

"And you haven't seen her since?"

"No! They only broke up from school a few weeks ago."

Amery looked at Merriweather, and then turned to Mr. and Mrs. Palmer. "Thank you for your co-operation, Mr. and Mrs. Palmer, Juliette, Jonathan. If we need anything else, we will be back in touch."

"Always ready to help, in any way we can!" said Mr. Palmer, rising from the settee and walking toward Amery, offering his hand, which Amery took and shook before leaving. Mr. Palmer showed them out, and they headed off toward the police station to interview the group assembled there. On the way, Merriweather and Amery talked about the interviews.

"Don't like the kid." said Amery. "Much too cocky for my liking! Make a note to check out his story, and find out when he left the gym."

They arrived at the police station around eight thirty am. A sergeant was at the desk and there were two 'erks' sitting on the bench. One was wearing a blue denim jacket done up to the neck and grey jeans with brown boots. The other had on a pair of light chinos, Nike trainers, tee-shirt and beige vee-neck jumper. They weren't talking to each other, and looked exceedingly sheepish.

Amery nodded to Johnson, who was sitting at a desk behind. He acknowledged him, nodded back, and moved behind the counter with Merriweather, who took a piece of paper from Johnson and passed on through into the interview room.

Amery took the paper from Merriweather and read the names and information off it. Turning to Merriweather, Amery said, "Ask Johnson to give you a DNA kit and bring it in here, and when you have it, tell the desk sergeant to bring in Stanley Withers."

Merriweather opened the door and crossed to Johnson, explaining what he wanted. Johnson found the kit and gave it to him, then Merriweather called to the desk sergeant, "Bring in Withers!"

The boy wearing the chinos, having heard his name being called, was looking at the desk sergeant, who motioned to him. The boy got up and moved through the room, as directed. He was handed over to Merriweather, who took him into the Interview room and told him to sit down at the table. He seemed very nervous and tense, but did what he was told.

Merriweather pushed the button on the recorder and said, "Tuesday twenty-eighth July nineteen ninety-eight. Eight twenty-five am, Newpark Police Station, jnterview with Stanley Withers. Present DS Merriweather."

Amery interposed, "and Detective Inspector

15

Amery."

"Well now, Stanley," - began Amery - "you are
only here to help us with our enquiries, so no need to get
nervous. You are not being charged with anything; you are
not being cautioned; you are just here to help us."

"You are eighteen years of age, so as an adult, I'm
sure you will understand why we need your help. You
seem like a nice lad, and I want to know first of all if you
would willingly give a sample of DNA and your
fingerprints, so we can eliminate you from the enquiry, and
all I want to know is where you were yesterday, and who
you saw. Now can you tell me that?"

Stanley relaxed a little in the chair and leaned
forward, "I haven't done anything, honest, guv'nor." he
started. "I'm happy to give you whatever you need, and I
didn't know about Sofia until this morning, when PC
Johnson came to the house."

"He said I should come here willingly to answer
some questions about her, so I came. I haven't got
anything to hide, and I've never been in any trouble with
the police."

Merriweather took the DNA kit from the table
and asked Stanley to open his mouth, while he swabbed it,
took a sample, and replaced the sample carefully in the
container provided with the kit, and he also took his
fingerprints for the file. He then placed the samples back
on the table.

Amery said in a very calm voice, "Just relax,

Stanley. Now just start at the beginning. Tell me exactly what you did yesterday, who you saw, where you went, and don't leave anything out. OK?"

"OK." said Stanley. "I got up at about nine forty-five am and had a cup of tea, got dressed and walked to the Mall. I got there about ten thirty. I met up with a couple of mates."

"Who?" interjected Amery.

"There was Brian Regan and Ronny Blenkinsop. We just talked about what we were going to do, which, before you ask," he added hastily "was to have a look around, and see if any of the girls we knew were there, and then see what was on at the cinema later in the afternoon."

He paused. "I remember seeing Sofia and Juliette about eleven o'clock, but can't be sure of the time, because I didn't look at my watch. I saw them in the restaurant having a drink, when the guys and I were walking past, and we just waved to them. I remember seeing Howard, but he only waved at us, as he was near the exit, and must have been on his way out, I think."

"So! Who is this, Howard? What's his surname?" asked Amery.

"Oh! Albanus. That's his surname. He's a bit of geek. Keeps to himself mostly, I see him around and we sort of know each other, but I don't hang around with him." Stanley answered.

"So why do you call him a geek, was it?" enquired

Amery.

"Well, he's into computers much more than any of us. We use them, of course we do. All of us have email accounts and search the web and play games, but he can fix computers, knows all about coding, and" - he paused for a short moment, then continued - "he knows how to make the games, you know? All that technical stuff. He doesn't come out with any of us, and I was really surprised to see him."

"Never seen him, or at least noticed him, at the Mall before. I didn't think it was his thing! If you get my drift?"

"And what did you do next?" Amery asked.

"We walked past the east exit, and I think we stopped at the carousel. There were some little kids on it, and I remember Brian saying the girls aren't here, so we went back toward the restaurant."

"Juliette was just leaving the restaurant and spoke to us. I remember asking her where Sofia was, as I saw her with her a few minutes earlier. Juliette said that Sofia had told her she was meeting someone and had to leave. I asked her who she was meeting, but Juliette said she didn't know."

"I remember we joked about that a lot, but I'm not sure what we said, because Sofia had never had a boyfriend that anyone knew of, so it seemed funny, but perhaps she wasn't meeting a boy. She never told Juliette, or at least Juliette never told us." He took a deep breath, and sank back into the chair for a few moments.

Amery studied him, then after a couple of seconds said, "And what did you do then?"

"Well, I think the three of us just walked around the Mall for a bit, and Juliette walked off; said she was going shopping. We saw a couple of the other guys."

"Who?" interjected Amery.

"There was Joshua Cleves, Obadiah Freeman and Samuel Tamarind. I'm sure I saw Juliette's brother Jonathan, but can't remember if that was before, or after I saw Juliette and Sofia in the restaurant."

"Were those three boys together?" Amery asked.

"Well, no. Josh and Obie were, and Samuel just happened to be there, I think." he replied.

"And what time do you think you saw them?" asked Amery.

"I saw Samuel about eleven am, and Josh and Obie about eleven thirty, but I can't be sure because I wasn't really thinking about time."

Amery gave Merriweather a knowing look, then asked Stanley, "How well do you know Jim Burton, the lad who was waiting with you outside?"

"I sort of know him but he's not one of my friends. I mean we were at the same high school, and I may have been in some of his classes, but I don't hang around with him. We've finished school a couple of weeks back and I've only got a month left, then I'm off to Uni in September, and I think he's doing an apprenticeship with his uncle."

"What sort?" Amery interjected again.

"His uncle owns the garage in town, so it makes sense, doesn't it? He loves cars and motorcycles, anything with a motor really, including women! - if you get my drift?"

"What do you mean by that, son? I don't get your drift!" retorted Amery.

"Oh! I mean, I mean, he's a good-looking bloke and the girls fall over themselves for him, don't they? He drives a car and he's got a motorbike. He's not one of your rich kids, but because his uncle owns the garage, he's always got access to one motor or another, and he's usually got some tasty bird on his arm, so to speak."

"Right!" said Amery giving him a little grin, then continued "Did you see him yesterday? Anywhere?" he asked him.

"No. I can't say I saw him at the Mall. I mean, it doesn't mean he wasn't there, just that I didn't see him. Of course, It could mean he wasn't there all day. I don't know. I'm sorry. PC Johnson asked me come here hours ago, and I'm bloody starving!"

"Do you mean you want something to eat, lad?" asked Amery.

"Yeah! I'm really hungry!" said Stanley. Amery turned to Merriweather. "Give the desk sergeant a shout for a sandwich and a cuppa for the lad."

"Oh!" he turned back to Stanley "Tea or coffee, milk and sugar?" he asked him. Stanley replied, "Cup of tea, please, and milk and sugar!"

Amery turned back to Merriweather "And get the kid outside a drink, too."

Merriweather turned to the tape and said, "DS Merriweather leaving the room at nine fifteen am." Then he left the tape running and went outside.

"What time did you leave the Mall?" Amery asked Stanley.

"It was about five thirty. We all left together and then I went home, and I guess that's what the others did."

Merriweather returned shortly, saying, "DS Merriweather, returning at nine twenty-five am."

"Here you are, lad." said Amery to Stanley, handing him the sandwich and cup of tea.

"Thanks!" said Stanley.

Amery signalled to Merriweather to stop the tape. Merriweather said, "Interview ended nine twenty-nine am." and switched the tape off.

They let Stanley eat his sandwich and drink his tea, then released him, telling him not to talk about the incident or the interview to anyone.

"We may need to talk to you again, Stanley, and if you remember anything else, you give us a call."

When Stanley left the interview room, Merriweather marked up the tape recording and put it into his pocket, then put a new one into the machine ready for the next interview. He placed the DNA kit, including the fingerprints, into a secure bag.

"Get Burton in, and find out if Johnson found any of the other kids we need to interview." Amery said to Merriweather. Now he was interested in talking to this Howard Albanus as well.

Merriweather left the room. He returned a few minutes later and said, "OK, guv, I've given the DNA kit and fingerprints to Johnson to get to forensics for comparison tests, and Johnson said he has collected two more of the local boys."

"He has brought in Joshua Cleves and Obadiah Freeman. They are waiting outside. Johnson says he's looking for Howard Albanus, but can't find him. But he's continuing to look, and he asks how many of these kids do you want to see?"

"Tell him I need to talk to Brian Regan, Ronnie Blenkinsop and Samuel Tamarind. Don't bring them in, just get me their addresses for the time being. Tell him to ask the lads outside if they would be willing to give DNA samples and fingerprints, to exclude them from our enquiries, and see what they say. If they agree, tell him to carry on and pass them onto forensics for comparisons, too."

"Ok, guv!" replied Merriweather.

Johnson brought in Jim Burton. Merriweather told him to sit down, which he did. Merriweather turned the tape on and said,

"Twenty eighth July, nineteen ninety-eight, nine forty-five am, Newpark Police Station. Interview with James Burton. Present, DS Merriweather." Amery said "and Detective Inspector Amery."

"Well, James," started Amery "or is it Jim? Which do you prefer?"

The boy shrugged his shoulders, replying, "I don't care, but Jim is better, I guess."

"OK, Jim it is. You seem like a nice lad, and I want to know if you would willingly give a sample of DNA and your fingerprints to exclude you from our investigation." Amery waited for him to reply.

"I'm happy to do that for you, but I don't know why. I haven't done anything wrong."

As soon as he agreed, Merriweather took the kit from the table behind him, swabbed James's throat and took his prints, which he did quite quickly, securing them safely, sealing them up and replacing them on the table behind him.

Amery continued as soon as Merriweather had

finished, "I know you've been waiting a long time but I'm sure you know about Sofia," - Burton nodded - "so, I've asked you here to see if you can help in my investigation. I need to find out where everyone was, and what everyone was doing. Do you understand? My job isn't easy, you know, and I could really do with your help."

Amery watched him, to observe any reactions he might have made, and continued, "So, tell me what you did yesterday. Everything you did, where you went, and who you saw."

"OK." said Jim. "I was at the garage at about eight thirty am. I work for my uncle Dave. He's my dad's brother and I've started my apprenticeship with him. I'm always there, and yesterday morning I was working in the garage on a BMW, and doing the pumps. My uncle was on the cash register in the office."

"OK, Jim." said Amery. "So, who did you see, and what happened for the rest of the day?"

"It was about five or ten past ten, or thereabouts, and I was on the pump. This bloke had asked me to fill his tank with diesel, and I saw Juliette waiting at the end of the forecourt. Then a few minutes later Sofia arrived."

"I finished filling this bloke's tank and told him how much it was, and he showed me a card, so I had to go into the office to get the card machine from my uncle. I took the machine out to the bloke, and he put his pin in, and then after the slip came out and I gave it to him, and he drove off. Sofia and Juliette were just walking away towards the Mall. That's all. I stayed at the garage till about five-thirty pm."

"Did you know the person whose car you were filling up?" asked Amery.

"Might have seen him around but not sure who he was." replied Burton.

"Did you get the registration number of the car, by any chance?" Amery asked.

"No. Sorry. It wasn't important." he replied, continuing "We may have it on the CCTV if Uncle switched it on!"

Amery made a mental note to find out if the CCTV had recorded the registration number and nodded to Merriweather, who knew what he wanted and wrote it in his pocketbook.

"Didn't you get a break at all, all day?" enquired Amery.

"Well, no!" said Jim. "Not sort of officially. I just ate my sandwiches and made a cup of tea or coffee whenever I wanted, which I did, and I really don't know what time it was, because I just went on working, but I did take the BMW for a test run about one forty-five, and I know that was the time because the clock in the car told me the time, and I remember looking at it, because of having changed the battery. I wanted to make sure it was working, so that's why I know what time it was!"

"Did you have to fill any other cars before you went for a test run?" asked Amery.

"Yes. Earlier in the morning before I took the BMW for a test run, Mrs. Palmer brought the blue Range Rover in about eleven-ish, and I filled that for her. She went into the office and paid, herself. Didn't even give me a tip!"

"So, Jim, what happened next?" Amery asked.

"I took the BMW out at about one forty-five, as I said before."

"Did you see anyone you knew, when you took the car for a test run?" Amery asked again.

"I wasn't really looking for people. I was concentrating on the car, listening to the engine and thinking about my driving, watching the road."

"So where did you drive?"

"I went through town, around the Mall car park, then out on the ring road, past the country park. I didn't go through the park, just around the ring road and back to the garage. Got back just before two-fifteen. I was only gone about thirty minutes."

"Enough time!" thought Amery.

"And are you sure you didn't see ANYBODY?" He stressed the last word.

"Funny you should say that, because I think I saw Howard. Don't know his other name. It was while I was driving round the ring road. Might have been about two-ish. I think it was him, anyway."

26

"What was he doing?" asked Amery.

"He was crossing the road from the park, towards west mall parking lot. But I didn't take a lot of notice, as I was more interested in the BMW." he replied.

"Did you notice if he was carrying anything?"

"I'm not sure. He might have been, but I wasn't really looking at him."

"Do you know if Howard owns a car?"

"He might. But I'm not too sure of that, either. He certainly doesn't bring it to my garage!"

"OK." said Amery. "You can go now, but we may need to talk to you again. Don't discuss this with anyone."

"Thank you." the lad replied, and added "I was sorry to hear about Sofia, she was a nice girl!"

"Interview ended ten twenty-five am." said Merriweather and switched the recorder off. He took out the tape, marked it up, and put it into his pocket with the other one from Stanley Withers, and gathered up the bag with the DNA samples he had put on the table.

"Right, Merry, let's talk to Cleaves and Freeman outside. We can always get them later if we need them. Did you get their addresses from Johnson?" he asked. Merriweather told him Johnson was putting a list of names and addresses together for him so he could collect them on their way out of the station, and could they find out if

Johnson had got the DNA samples from them?

"Then, I think, you and I, Merry had better drive round this town a bit more, before taking those tapes to be typed up!" said Amery.

"Good idea, guv!" said Merriweather, and together they left the room.

The two lads were sitting waiting on the bench, and stood up as Amery and Merriweather approached them.

"Which one of you is Joshua?" asked Amery, and one of the lads immediately replied "That's me, sir."

"Right." He turned "So, you are Obadiah Freeman?" and the other boy nodded. "Well, just need to know, for now, at what time you arrived at the Mall!" Both boys answered together "About eleven thirty."

"And what time did you leave?"

Obadiah said, "Around five." and Joshua agreed "Yes, that's about right."

"OK, boys. Have you given your DNA and fingerprints to the office here?" Amery asked them. They nodded. "Well, I'm going to let you go home now, but I may need to talk to you both later, so don't talk about this to anyone, and don't leave town!" and he laughed. The boys smiled and left the police station.

Johnson took the samples from Merriweather, and said he would pass them, and the samples from the two

boys, on to forensics for comparison, and did
Merriweather want to give him the tapes? He could get
them to DC Thomas at the mobile unit for typing up.
Merriweather was very happy to pass them on.

CHAPTER THREE

CCTV

Before Amery and Merriweather left the police station, Johnson handed Merriweather a sheet containing the names and addresses of the people that Amery had requested. Merriweather drove as Amery had directed, around the ring road, then back to the mall car park. They left the car and entered by the east entrance. Making their way around, they saw how the various shops, cinema and restaurant were located near the west entrance and exit. They left the mall, and found they were opposite the county park. They walked through the car park and crossed the road to the park.

"So, if we believe what James Burton told us, it was around here that he thought Howard Albanus might have come out of the park at about two o'clock and crossed to the mall car park!" Amery said. "So let's just have a little look around here, and see if there is anything that might connect to Sofia's murder. Even though it's about a mile to the other side of the park, where her body was found."

The two experienced detectives gingerly studied the area. Walking a few feet into the park, but not wanting to disturb evidence, if there was any, they stared keenly into the undergrowth. It didn't take long before Amery shouted to Merriweather,

"Here! I think I've found a bag." Merriweather crossed over to him and marked the ground with a pencil from his pocket.

"You got any evidence bags in your pocket, Merry?" asked Amery.

"You know, guv, I have everything in my pockets!" And with that he took out a pair of disposable gloves and an evidence bag. Putting on the gloves, he picked up the bag and put it into the evidence bag, sealed it and wrote on it, the time, date, and place it was found. He then made a note in his pocketbook to show the area they were in, and its proximity to the mall.

Having done that, Amery said, "I think we'll get SOCO out here to have a thorough look!" and with that he took out his own phone and made a call, saying they would wait for them to arrive.

When SOCO arrived, Merriweather handed over the evidence bag and pointed out where it was found. Amery told them they were looking for any other items that might have belonged to the victim, or any footprints.

"You know your job, boys, so I'll leave it up to

you. Call me later, and you can update me!"

Amery and Merriweather then walked back across the road, through the car park, through the mall, and back to the east entrance and to their car.

"Where to now, guv?" asked Merriweather, starting the engine.

"Before we interview Howard Albanus, I want to go to that gym and make some enquiries there."

Merriweather put the car in gear, released the clutch gently, hit the accelerator and drove off. Amery made mental notes of the views as they passed through the town, passed the garage and fire station, passing by some of the houses and arriving at the gym, swimming pool, and recreational centre.

"It's pretty impressive!" he thought, as the car pulled into a parking space.

They got out of the car and walked into the gym, and up to the reception desk, where a pretty young woman about twenty-six years old was seated.

"Can I help you?" she asked.

Amery took out his warrant card and showed it to her, saying, "We need to talk to someone in charge, and do you have CCTV here?"

She replied quickly. "I'll call Andy, he's the manager."

Then she picked up the intercom and announced, "Would the manager report to the front desk, please?" Returning to her conversation with Amery, she replied, "We do have CCTV everywhere in here, except for the changing and shower rooms, and we also have it for the car park."

"Good!" said Amery. "Do people have to sign in when they arrive?"

"Yes." she replied "but they don't actually physically sign in. They swipe their membership card on the reader." She pointed to the electronic system near the entrance. "Then they do the same thing when they leave. It's recorded on our computers, so we can tell who uses the facilities, and for how long."

"What happens if they don't register their card? Can they still use the facilities?" asked Amery.

"No. Well, they could get a coffee from the coffee shop, or watch the swimming pool and gym from the gallery, but they wouldn't be able to get into the gym or swimming pool through the doors, unless someone opened it for them, which is unlikely. The card has to be swiped to open it, so to speak, and all the gym equipment needs the card to register them. Also, the trainers would question them if they weren't using their membership card."

As she finished speaking, the double doors leading through into the main gym and pool areas opened, and a tall, muscular, tanned young man of about thirty-five came through.

"Hi, Pat, what do you need me for? Oh, hello, gentlemen!" he said, as he saw Amery and Merriweather standing behind her. "How can I help you?"

Amery produced his warrant card, restating their introduction. The young man introduced himself as Andy, saying he was the manager. Amery asked if there were somewhere private they could meet, upon which the young man took them back through the double doors and into an office, where there were various CCTV monitors.

"I'm glad we've come in here." said Amery. "This might help us in our enquiries."

"Anything to help. Can I give you a coffee or a cold drink?" asked Andy.

"That would be good." said Amery, and he turned to Merriweather. "Coffee for you, too?" Merriweather nodded.

Andy picked up the phone on his desk, waited a few seconds and said into it, "Pat, organise three coffees to my office, please!" then put the phone down.

"How can I help you?" he asked Amery. Merriweather already had his pocketbook out, and was writing in it.

"I need to know about one of your members. He tells me he was here yesterday, from early in the morning until three pm, or thereabouts. He said he used the gym and the swimming pool, and I need to check this!"

Andy beamed and said, "Our computer system

should be able to tell when he checked in and checked out. It should also tell us what equipment he used in the gym, and when he went into the swimming pool, and what time he left the building. We might be able to look at the CCTV too!"

He was very proud of their system, having been involved in its installation.

Amery moved across the room to the computer and stood behind Andy as he opened the system. "What is the name of the member?" he asked.

"Jonathan Palmer." Andy replied, and gave him his address too.

"Right!" said Andy. "According to this, he checked in at about eight thirty am. He went to the gym and used the treadmill at eight forty-five. Then at nine oh five he used one of the rowing machines, and at nine forty-five he moved onto the elliptical machine, otherwise known as the cross-trainer. These machines are all cardiovascular machines."

"He then moved onto the resistance machines and used hack squat, leg extension, leg curl, seated calf, the peck deck and chest press. He appeared to finish on the treadmill again for a cooldown about eleven fifteen. He must have gone to shower, because I can't see him registering for anything for while! He next appears going into the swimming pool at two thirty pm."

That's really strange! I can't see him registering anywhere on here! He hasn't checked out but he's not registering!"

The door opened and the young woman came in carrying a tray with three disposable cups of coffee, sachets of sugar, milk and wooden spoons.

"Just put them on the desk, Pat. Thank you!" Andy said, and looked at Amery, who was looking puzzled, too.

"Can we look at the CCTV between those hours?" he asked Andy.

The young woman put the tray down and left the room. Merriweather put his pocketbook in his pocket and picked up one of the coffees, added some sugar, stirred it with the wooden stick, then put it to his lips and sipped it. He then took another of the coffees, and passed it to Amery while he watched what was going on.

Andy moved across to the computer near the monitors and hit some keys on it. The monitors flashed off, then on again, and rewound the images very quickly.

He stopped the film and said, "Right, sir, these are the monitors from the gym, swimming pool, coffee shop, and car park from eleven ten am yesterday!"

Merriweather and Amery watched the monitors. They could see Jonathan on the treadmill, wearing grey jogging bottoms, grey tee-shirt and sneakers, and with the sweat pouring down his face and back, making large wet stains on his tee-shirt.

"Andy, can you speed it up to eleven fifteen when

he finishes on here? I want to see where he goes!" asked Amery.

"Sure!" replied Andy, as he pressed fast forward, and all the monitors moved faster, showing everyone's images speeded up.

Although they were in fast forward, they continued to watch Jonathan stop the treadmill, get off, and quickly go into the changing room, where the showers and toilet facilities were. Of course there was no CCTV in there, but Andy kept the images fast forwarding, and watched the clock on the screen showing eleven twenty, thirty, forty, fifty, then,

"Stop!" shouted Amery, and Andy freeze-framed the images.

"Look, Merriweather, look at the car park. Isn't that him getting into that red car?"

"It bloody well is!" exclaimed Merriweather. "What is he wearing, governor? Looks like he has the same sports stuff on."

"Now, how did he get out of the building from the changing room, without coming through the building?" Amery asked, continuing "We need to look at your changing rooms, but before we do that I want to see if he returns!"

So Andy continued to run the video in fast forward until the clock showed two fifteen. They saw Jonathan's car pull back into the car park, and Jonathan get out and run behind the building.

Then, at two twenty-five, he appeared, coming out of the changing room door leading to the swimming pool, wearing swimming trunks. He stepped through the foot bath and dived into the water. He swam two lengths of the baths, then got out and walked back into the changing room.

He appeared again at two fifty, dressed in chinos and jumper, and wearing sneakers. He climbed the stairs to the coffee shop.

They saw him chat to the girl behind the counter as she passed him a coffee in a disposable cup, which he drank from, then discarded into the trash bin. He then left the building through the main doors, at three pm.

Amery took a huge gulp of his coffee then said, "We need to look at your changing room, Andy, and I need all these videos or whatever you have!" as he finished his coffee and threw the cup into the waste bin. Merriweather did the same.

"Of course! I'll get them for you straight away!" said Andy, as he busily set about on the keyboard. "I'll put the recordings onto a flash drive. I'll leave it downloading while I show you the changing rooms. I need to see how people can get in and out without the system knowing, as well!" he said, as he stepped toward his desk and picked up his coffee, which by now was cold.

He put it down, then said, "They are this way!" Using a swipe card as he opened doors, he led them out of the office through another set of doors and into one of the changing rooms.

"This is the one that Jonathan used, is it?" Amery questioned Andy, while looking at the room.

Rows of wooden benches ran through the centre of the room, with hooks for hanging clothes above them on a frame. There were a few items of clothing on one or two of the hooks, and a couple of bags under the benches. There was a row of lockers on one wall, at the end of which were two doors, one marked 'To the Swimming Pool' and the other 'To the Gym'.

There was a long mirror with a counter or worktop under, running the length of the other wall. An opening at the end of the wall led to a bank of six showers to the right. To the left stood a wall of urinals, and opposite to them were six cubicles with toilets.

Amery pushed each toilet door open, but the last door was locked, and not a cubicle at all.

"What's this?" Amery immediately asked Andy.

"It's part of the power system and pump room. You'll need a key to get in."

"Hang on!" he said, as he ran back to his office, returning a few moments later with a key.

He opened the door and Amery stepped in. It was a short tunnel which opened up to exactly what he had said; a pump room with equipment for the swimming pool, and at the end a fire door, which opened on a push bar.

"That's how he did it!" said Amery to Merriweather. "But how did he get a key for that door?" he queried.

"I don't know! I have no idea, but I'd better change the lock." Andy replied.

They went back into the changing room, and Amery examined the lockers. "Can members use any of these lockers?"

"Some members have their own, which they pay an annual fee for. It's usually the more dedicated members, those who come at least four times a week. It saves them bringing a change of clothes; they can store their valuables safely, and they are certain they will get a locker, even when it's really busy. They don't need towels, as you can see, we have clean towels here for members' use and a bin to put used ones in."

"Does Jonathan have one of these?" questioned Amery.

"I will check for you." Andy replied, and again he went to his office, returning a few minutes later.

"Yes, it's number twenty-four. And before you ask, I've brought the pass key. Members know that we have a pass key, which is primarily in case they lose their key, but they know that we can open their lockers from time to time, to check their contents and ensure there are no illegal or illicit items or literature. We have high standards, even though we are in the recreation industry. Anyway, you can open it, if you want."

"I think you had better open it, Andy, and we'll look inside!"

Dutifully, Andy opened locker number twenty four, and immediately Amery saw the grey jogging bottoms, tee-shirt and grey sweatshirt that Jonathan had been wearing when he had left the gym and returned at two fifteen pm. There was also a pair of swimming trunks, hanging on a hook inside the door.

"Do you want me to take them out?" Andy asked.

Amery replied, "NO! Definitely not. Do not touch anything!" and turned to Merriweather "Any more gloves in your pockets?

"Sorry, guv!" was the reply.

"Andy," said Amery "can you seal this room off? I mean, can you lock it so no one, and I mean no one, can use it?"

Andy replied, "Well I can, but if any of our clients are here now, they may have their clothes in here!" He looked at Amery. "What do you suggest I do?" he asked.

"OK, Andy. First, you lock this up and secure the key!" Amery pointed to the locker. "Next, you tell everyone, over your public address system, that there is a problem with this changing room, and they should come immediately and collect their belongings and use the other changing room. DC Merriweather will stay here with you until everyone who has anything comes in and then leaves, and then we need to lock this changing room up, and I need your assurance that no one, not even you, will re-enter! I'll get someone down here PDQ to check out that locker. OK, Andy?"

"Yes, sir!" Andy replied, and left the changing room.

A few moments later he announced over the public address system that there had been a burst pipe in changing room one, and any gentlemen who had left any property in there needed to collect it immediately, because the room was to be sealed off for health and safety reasons, and that no one would be able to enter thereafter until further notice, continuing, "Gentlemen, members, and guests can use Changing Room Two."

He returned to the changing room. Amery left, with him, returning to Andy's office. Merriweather and Andy waited until three men arrived at the changing room and collected clothes from hooks, picking up some bags. One other chap opened up a locker. He took out some clothing and a backpack, into which he put the clothing and a pair of shoes, then he left the changing room. Andy said "I think that's all of them!"

"OK!" said Merriweather. "Now I want all those doors locked up like the Tower of London!" and he laughed.

After they had locked all the internal doors, they left the changing room. Andy locked that door also, as they had asked him to do, and said to Merriweather, "Do you want the key, sir?"

"I don't think so, Andy. I think we can trust you to lock that key away safely, together with the locker key, until we return, or someone comes to give it a going-over!"

They went back into Andy's office, where Amery was sitting patiently waiting, and seemingly deep in thought. Andy went over to the computer, examined it, then removed the flash drive and handed it to Amery.

"How long do you think I will have to keep that changing room locked? I need to check the pumps and mixtures for the swimming pool every day!"

"Not sure, I'm afraid, but we will be as quick as we can! I'm hoping it won't be more than a couple of days." replied Amery.

"OK." said Andy. "I'll make sure that I'm on duty all the time, so I won't have to tell anyone else what's going on."

"Well done!" said Amery. "That would be a great help."

"I'll tell the other staff the same thing - about a burst pipe. I'll tell them I've switched the water off, so no one can use the room at all for health and safety reasons."

"If they say they want to test the pH in the pool, then I'll tell them they have to do it the old-fashioned way, and dip the water. That will keep them busy, and that should cover everything! At least for a day or two."

"Here is my card." he said, handing it to Amery. "If you need to call me, this is my direct line." He pointed at one of the numbers on the card. "And this one is my mobile phone number."

"OK, Andy, thank you for your co-operation!" He rose, taking the card, and shook hands. Then he and Merriweather left.

Returning to their car in the car park, Amery said, "Don't know about you, Merry, but I'm starving! Let's try out that restaurant in the Mall, and we can check if they have any CCTV, but first I want to see if Control has the tapes, and to see how the typist is doing with them." So Merriweather drove back to the mobile unit, where the civilian typist was waiting.

While Amery waited in the car, Merriweather went into the unit and asked her if she had received the tapes from PC Johnson. She replied that she had, and she was working her way through them.

He told her they were going to the mall to carry out some more investigations, and if needed, she could contact him on his mobile. He then handed her his card and told her that DC Peter Thomas should arrive at the unit in the immediate future, but under no circumstance should she go and leave the mobile unit unattended.

He then told her that there might be a couple of other detectives arriving at some point, and she might know them from the area, and that DC Thomas would be the office manager, and collate all the information as it came in. But she need not wait for DI Amery, or him, to return.

He left the unit, returned to the car and drove off to the mall again, this time parking on the east side.

It was now gone three pm and neither had eaten, so going to the restaurant was not only an opportunity to examine the view from the restaurant, but the right time to fill an empty belly and have a quick pint of beer. Having examined the menu, both Amery and Merriweather ordered a burger with chips and a pint of their finest ale, which arrived very promptly.

"I needed that!" said Amery, taking the first gulp of the beer.

"Me too!" responded Merriweather. Their food arrived within ten minutes and while they ate, they talked about the case to date.

"I've put in a call to the Chief Constable about that locker, and instructed the forensic guys to go through it." said Amery, continuing "I made the call while you were in the unit."

"I was concerned that we didn't want to make an illegal search without a warrant, but the Chief tells me that if the manager of the centre has permission to go through it, and he has the key, then there is nothing to stop us doing the same with his permission. Hence the call to SOCO."

"I gave the lad at the gym a call to tell them they were on their way, and they will let me know what they find, and what I want to do with any evidence."

"From here," said Merriweather "you have a good view of the west entrance and exit, so anyone sitting here can see who comes and goes, if they cared to!" Amery waved a hand to the waitress who came over to them.

"Do you have CCTV in here?" he asked.

"No, sorry, but the centre has cameras all over the place. Some of the shops have it, but who would want to steal anything from a restaurant?" she asked, sardonically.

"Where is the Centre Manager's office?" he asked her.

"Through there!" She pointed towards the corridor leading to the west entrance. "Towards the west exit, then just past the toilets, there is a staircase on the left. That will take you there. If you look up there," she said, pointing above the entrance to the corridor, "you can see her office."

They looked up and could see the large glass windows spanning over the corridor.

"Thanks!" said Amery. "Can you bring us our bill please?"

"Together, or separate bills?" she asked.

"One bill, thanks!" he said. "I'll need a receipt." She walked off.

Both Merriweather and Amery looked up at the

window again, then looked to the left and right of the mall.

"I wonder how many of these shops have CCTV in them?" Merriweather queried.

"Perhaps the management of this place will know. I can see cameras all over this place, so her office is a good place to start." Amery answered.

Amery paid the bill and left a twenty per cent tip, which didn't show on the receipt that he had pocketed before he got up from the table. Merriweather took a last gulp of his beer and followed him. The two walked down the corridor and went up to the management office. They noticed a security spy-hole in the locked door and knocked on it. They held their warrant cards up for inspection through the spy-hole and waited a few moments, before the door opened with a click.

An extremely pretty young woman entered. She was in her late thirties and had dark red hair, neatly tied back. She wore a smart business suit.

"How can I help you, gentlemen?" she asked. Amery formally introduced himself and Merriweather.

"Do come in!" the young woman said, as she opened the door fully, for them to enter a short corridor. "My name is Cassidy. Julia Cassidy. I am the Centre Manager. Please come into my office and tell me how can I help you!"

They entered the room. Amery went immediately to the window to ascertain what could actually be seen from there. Merriweather stood just inside the door.

The view wasn't as much as Amery had hoped for, but he could certainly see the restaurant, about four of the shops to the right of it, and about the same to the left. He could see a vendor selling something-or-other on a mobile stall in the middle of the walkway, and several people walking, talking and generally mingling around the mall. He couldn't see as far as the east side of the mall.

He turned to Julia and said, "I understand you have CCTV."

She was puzzled, but replied, "Yes, we have cameras all over the Mall! They are monitored in the control room just through here."

She opened the door next to the window. Walking in, they followed her, immediately noticing the monitors showing many areas of the mall. There was another door on the other side of the room, which they thought must lead to the corridor they had just entered by. There were also two men in grey uniforms.

One was watching the screens, and the other was just rising and moving towards the door. He stopped and turned as they entered, looking across at Julia and the detectives.

"Do you keep CCTV recordings of the mall?" Amery asked Julia, but he was looking at the two men.

The man near the door replied, "Yes! We usually keep the recording for up to fourteen days, or if there has been a theft or an incident that might require evidence, and we have captured it on CCTV. We keep the recordings as long as is necessary."

Julia asked, "Is there something in particular you are looking for?"

Amery replied, "We are looking to confirm the whereabouts of some people that we understand were here yesterday, between ten thirty am and three thirty pm."

The man close to the door moved back to the monitors, and said, "If you come around here, I can play the recordings for you. It might take some time, as we have twenty cameras around the Mall, but all the records are here."

Amery and Merriweather crossed the room and pulled up a couple of chairs. The other man continued to monitor the other cameras which were focussing on that day's activities.

Julia said, "Would you like some coffee or tea brought in? I think you might be some time!"

Merriweather replied, "Not for me, thank you! Not right now." Amery just shook his head with a smile.

The man who was showing them the tapes told them his name was Dave, and that he had worked there yesterday. He had heard about the murder, and would help in any way he could.

Amery and Merriweather spent almost three hours watching the various recordings, which showed the many entries and exits of people shopping and walking around, some stopping to talk in the various areas of the mall.

Also, there were timings on the recordings! Merriweather made copious notes with times. They noticed a young man who was on his own. He was tall with blond hair. He appeared to come into the mall by the east entrance, walk through, and leave through the west corridor, at eleven fifteen. They couldn't get a close-up of his face, but he had blond hair which was quite distinctive, and he wore dark blue denim jeans and a blue jumper.

They watched Sofia and Juliette sitting in the restaurant, and they saw Sofia leave at eleven twenty-nine via the west entrance. They saw Stanley Withers with two other young men, guessing they were Regan and Blenkinsop speaking to Juliette at eleven thirty, confirming what Withers had told them. They saw Cleves and Freeman and another olive-skinned young man, whom they assumed was Samuel Tamarind, though the three did not appear together.

Then, surprisingly, they saw Jonathan Palmer at eleven thirty-three. He came in via the east entrance, appeared to look around, and left by the same entrance a few minutes later at eleven thirty-six, followed by the young man they had assumed was Samuel Tamarind. The clock registered eleven thirty-eight as he also left via the east entrance.

Amery asked Dave to switch to the tapes for the east car park between eleven am and one pm. Again, Merriweather kept notes and watched, as various cars came in and went out of the car park, and people went in and out of the mall, then the red car.

They had seen Jonathan Palmer driving up to the gym, pulling into the car park at eleven thirty. He drove to the edge of the car park, to a shaded area where there were trees and bushes. He parked the car and got out.

He was wearing a pair of grey jogging bottoms and sweatshirt, with sneakers. He walked into the east entrance, entering at eleven thirty-three, where the inside camera picked him up. He was only out of shot, from the car park videocamera's viewpoint, for approximately three minutes, before he reappeared at eleven thirty-six. He crossed towards the car park, stopped, turned, and waited.

At eleven thirty-eight, the young man they had assumed was Samuel Tamarind appeared from the east entrance, stopped, looked around and then walked on toward Palmer. The two of them chatted, then walked to Palmer's car. They appeared to be looking around. Then Palmer's car lights flashed, a sign he was unlocking his car, and the two both got into the back seat of the car.

Neither Amery, Merriweather, or Dave could see inside the vehicle, but once again Amery asked for the tape to be fast-forwarded. He then asked for it to be stopped thirty minutes later, when at twelve oh eight, Palmer got out of the rear door of his car and, closing it, opened the front door of the car, got in and drove off. The other lad did not get out of the car.

Amery asked to see the west car park and the monitors were switched, rewound and, when the clock on the monitor registered eleven am, started to play at regular speed. Amery asked him to speed the tape up to eleven fifteen, which he did, then stopped and played it at regular speed.

From the angle of the camera, Amery could see the car park, the ring road, and the edge of the park. The young man with blond hair, who wore dark blue denim jeans and blue jumper, appeared from the west entrance. They watched him walk through the car park, across the road, and into the park.

"So!" said Amery to Merriweather. "I'm assuming that is Howard Albanus we're watching." As he spoke, the boy disappeared into the park opposite. "Fast forward, will you? To eleven twenty-five." said Amery.

"OK." Dave replied, and the monitor flashed forward until the clock showed eleven twenty-five. They could see that a few people were parking cars, and going in and coming out of the mall, some carrying bags of shopping, and others just walking in and out.

Then at eleven thirty, they saw Sofia come out of the mall and walk across the car park, into the park opposite.

"Can you fast forward to about two pm?" asked Amery.

"Yeah, no problem!" and with that the images flashed forward quickly.

Amery and Merriweather continued watching the screens and suddenly Amery said, "Stop!"

The clock registered twelve-fifty pm.

"Just go back a few minutes for me, and stop!" He turned to Merriweather and said, "It's the red car!"

Merriweather noted it down as Palmer's car had returned to the other car park. Having left from the east at twelve oh eight, he was now arriving back at the west car park at twelve forty-five pm. Amery asked for the tape to be played at normal speed and watched as the car was parked. The driver, Jonathan Palmer, got out of the driver's door and a passenger got out of the nearside door.

This looked like the same boy who was in the back of the car when Palmer drove out of the carpark at twelve oh eight. The two left the car and walked across the road to the park.

"OK, lets fast forward again, but can we go just a little slower, please?" Amery asked, and Dave smiled and started the images going in fast forward, but a little slower.

Intently concentrating on the images, they watched people loading cars and driving out, and others arriving, parking, and walking in. As the images approached one fifty pm, Amery asked for them at normal speed and, as Burton had said in his interview, out of the park appeared Howard Albanus again, stopping to let a BMW go past him before he crossed to the carpark.

"Stop the film!" said Amery again. "Can we zoom in on him?" He pointed to Albanus on the screen.

"I'll try," replied Dave "but this is a recording. It

isn't live, so I might not be able to."

He tried to enlarge the image. "I'm sorry I can't, but your people might be able to enhance the image because I think they have the specialist gear."

Amery and Merriweather peered at the screen. They were looking to study his clothing. Was it damaged, or dirty in any way? Did it look very different from when he went into the park?

They couldn't be sure, so they asked Dave to continue. They watched Abanus as he crossed to his car. He appeared to be holding his arm around himself. Was he carrying something under his jumper?

They couldn't be sure, but they watched as Albanus got into a dark blue or black Ford Escort and drove out of the car park.

"Can you recognize the registration on that?" asked Amery.

"Probably, as we have a number plate recognition system, so I just need to see the time he leaves, and I'll find it for you." replied Dave.

He stopped the film, crossed to another monitor, and then returned with a number written on a piece of paper: 'N121 HOW'.

"Thank you!" said Amery. "Let's continue!"

When the clock registered one fifty-nine pm, out of the park appeared Palmer and the same other young man, whom they were still assuming was Tamarind.

They crossed to the carpark and Palmer shook the other boy's hand. Palmer got in his car and drove out, while the other boy went back into the mall via the west entrance.

"Just go to the inside of the mall, will you Dave?" asked Amery. Dave switched the camera so that they now saw Tamarind appear, entering the mall.

They could see he had dirty hands, and looked a bit dishevelled. He went directly into the toilets and came back out eight minutes later. He appeared to have tidied himself up a little, and he was rubbing his hands as if they weren't quite dry, and he had tucked in his shirt. He walked off, down the corridor and into the main mall.

"I think I've seen enough for now, thanks, Dave!" said Amery as he turned to Merriweather, who took a deep breath and blew it out noisily.

"I need you to secure all these tapes or videos, and hold them, as I will definitely need them later. And probably for the rest of yesterday. Thank you for your help, and that's all I need for now!"

He asked where Julia was, and Dave told him she was in her office. Amery and Merriweather knocked on the internal door and walked in, without waiting for her to open it.

She was sitting behind her desk, appearing to be working with some papers scattered on her desk, but she looked up as they walked in.

"I want to thank you for your co-operation!" started Amery. "Do you have a card so I can contact you later?" he asked her with a smile.

She smiled back at him, opened a drawer on her desk and took out a business card.

"Feel free to call me anytime." she said, handing it to him, smiling. There was a sparkle in her eye.

Amery smiled back and took the card, ensuring he touched her hand as he took it, and he and Merriweather left. Walking back to their car, Merriweather commented on her good looks and gave Amery a knowing look. Nothing else was said.

It was now just after seven pm when they arrived back at the mobile unit. There were two cars already parked outside. The civilian secretary was still there, along with DC Thomas.

"Glad to see you, Peter!" Amery said to DC Thomas. "Got lots of info we need to collate, and we need to do some more interviews." He continued "But first I need to know if SOCO have got back with any information." He turned to the young woman.

"Have you typed up those tapes for me, lass?" he asked her, and she handed him several typewritten sheets. "Thank you!"

He hesitated, then added "What's your name?"

"Corinna Watson." she replied, then added "There have been a couple of calls for you. I left the notes on here." She pointed to a pin board on the wall.

"Thank you! You'd better run off now, and be back at nine in the morning. OK?"

"Great, thank you! I'll see you tomorrow." she said, acknowledging them all, and with that she left.

Amery, Merriweather and Thomas sat down. Amery was behind his desk. Merriweather and Thomas sat on a couple of chairs in front of it.

"OK. It's been a busy day, but we now need to follow up and see what information we have." Amery started. "Peter, you need to get this information together! Merry has made notes and will get them typed up for you. We have the statements from our investigation, which so far seem to be accurate, and we've watched various video evidence. Here is a flash drive from the gym, showing a distinct time-line we can follow."

"The Shopping Mall has video evidence which Merry and I have seen - and that was very interesting. We can get copies of them anytime, but I think Merry has made some notes of people, places, and times, so you can use them to confirm times of movement of the potential or possible suspects in this case."

"Have we got the reports from SOCO yet?" he enquired.

Peter replied, "I understand forensics have

finished at the scene, and a wider sweep of the area has been made. Another shoe was found, and drag marks indicating that she was dragged from A to B, where she died. No other items of her clothing were found."

"There were various footprints and paw prints around the scene, and we are still awaiting the results of the DNA testing, but the forensic report and post-mortem findings are on your desk."

"I believe the medical examiner/pathologist already gave you a verbal report of his findings. SOCO have reported that they have investigated and examined the locker at the gym. There was a pair of swimming trunks hanging on the inside of the door of the locker and a man's clothing was found in the locker, consisting of jogging pants and a tee-shirt."

"Semen was on the pants, and they have been taken for DNA testing. They swabbed the locker and its contents. As I said, there was only clothing, but it is all bagged and tagged, and prints were also taken from the inside of the locker. We await those results."

"That info was from a telephone call, and the reports should be here by tomorrow morning, but the DNA will take longer, probably ten to twelve days!"

"Regarding the bag that you found in the park; it was empty, and it would appear that it did not belong to the victim. There was no evidence on it for us to presume that it did, however we still await the DNA."

"WPC Scott reported at five thirty pm that she is

no longer staying with the family, and has gone home, but she will return to support the family tomorrow. There is a police presence outside for their security and privacy."

"Thanks, Peter, that just threw a spanner in the works. I would have loved that bag to have been hers, and evidence in it."

Amery paused for thought for a moment. Merry and Thomas watched him. Then he said, "Right, well, I don't think there is much we can do now. It's gone eight pm. I think we all need a good night's sleep and another early start."

"We need to map a time-line with the evidence we have, and see where that takes us. We have some of the suspects with gaps in their stories that need to be examined further, and there are still a couple of people we need to interview and some we need to re-interview, so let's call it a night for now and meet back here at eight am."

He rose, picked his briefcase up from the floor, placed it on the table, opened it, picked up some papers from his desk, placed them inside, and closed the case, replacing it back on the floor where he left it. He walked around his desk. Merriweather and Thomas also rose, and the three of them exited the unit.

Thomas locked the door and told them that he had confirmed that the local police would ensure a uniformed twenty-four-hour police presence for the unit.

CHAPTER FOUR

AMERY

It was around eight forty-five pm when Amery arrived home. He was living in a small, detached house that had once been his family home. His wife had died two years earlier. They had been married for four years, had no children and led a nice comfortable life. Expensive and exciting holidays abroad. Ski-ing in the winter in Austria. Florida or the Caribbean in the summer, when he could get the time off. She'd been a high-flyer in the city. No glass ceiling for her!

They had met at a mutual friend's wedding and there'd been an instant attraction. They'd only known each other for six months, but found they had so much in common, enjoying so much together, that they decided to get married. They knew they loved each other, and nothing was going to stand in their way of their future happiness together.

But four years on, suddenly, and from nowhere, she had become unwell, and within a month she was gone. They said the cause was a faulty heart valve with complications, and there was nothing anyone could have done about it. It wasn't something that could easily have been detected. Anyway, now he lived alone, and had concentrated his life on his work.

Since then he had felt no feeling for women, but today something about Julia stirred within him. She looked attractive; she was smartly dressed and intelligent. He thumbed her business card through his fingers and worried whether it was too late to call her.

The clock read eight fifty-five as he picked up the phone and called her number. She answered after a couple of rings.

"Hello?" was all she said.

"Hi Julia. I hope it's not too late to call you. I was wondering if you fancied meeting up sometime? Oh! By the way, it's Inspector Amery. Simon. We met this afternoon."

He felt really clumsy. It had been a long time since he had asked anyone for a date, and he wasn't sure if that was what he'd actually just done!

"Hi, Simon. Thanks for calling. I was hoping you would, and yes, I'd love to meet up sometime! In fact I've not been home long, and I'm not sure how far away from me you are, but I was actually thinking of going for a drink right now."

"Where are you?" he asked her.

She told him where she was and they arranged to meet at nine thirty at The Duke's Head in Park Manor. It was about twenty minutes away from his place and, from what she said, about the same distance for her.

He ran upstairs, jumped in the shower, changed his clothes, and was out of the house by ten past nine. He drove to The Duke's Head, parked his car near the exit to the parking lot and walked into the lounge bar, where he saw her sitting at the bar.

She turned as he opened the door, and the evening breeze blew in. She was wearing a bright red skirt and top with a short cropped black velvet jacket, and wore stockings or tights and very high heeled red shoes. She sat with her left leg crossed over her right, straight-backed, with her dark red hair hanging down over her shoulder.

He smiled and strolled over to her. He hadn't been dating for such a long time that he wasn't sure whether he should shake her hand or kiss her. Throwing caution to the wind, he kissed her on the cheek and said, "Julia, it's really nice to see you, and I'm glad you agreed to meet me!"

She smiled at him and asked what he wanted to drink, as she already had a glass in front on her. Amery replied, "I'll have a whisky and soda. I think I need it after the day I've had!" They laughed together.

The barman came over to them and she ordered his drink. When it arrived, they took their glasses and moved to a secluded table in the corner of the room.

"I'm really sorry!" he said. "I didn't ask you if you wanted to eat something. I wouldn't mind a little something myself. I'm not sure when I last ate!" and he laughed again, thinking of the burger and chips he had eaten at the mall just before he met her.

"Do you know, I think I could manage something! I've been so busy today. With these policemen coming in and looking through all my videos, it's been really time-consuming!" she replied, laughing again.

Amery waved his hand, and the waiter came over to their table. "Is it too late to get something to eat - we're bloody starving!" He tried to look pathetically at the waiter.

"No. You're all right mate, but make a quick decision, before the chef closes the kitchen!" said the waiter as he handed them the menu.

After its inspection, Amery ordered steak and chips. Julia ordered coronation chicken and salad. Both arrived within twenty minutes, during which time they talked about the weather, the news headlines, and her work.

He enjoyed her company. She was intelligent, which he liked in a woman. She had ambition, and she was quite beautiful. When the bill came she offered to pay, which he liked. But he paid, and he left the tip. He walked her to her car and arranged to meet her again, saying he would have to call to arrange when, as he was really tied up with this murder, right at that moment.

He put his arm around her waist and pulling her close to him, gently kissed her on the lips. Not passionately, but more than just friends. She responded likewise, gently putting her arm around his neck and running her fingers through his hair. As he released his gentle hold, he opened the door of her car and held it while she climbed in.

"I will call you soon," he said "I promise!" She smiled at him as he closed the door of her car, and replied,"I hope so." before she put the car in gear, and drove out of the car park.

He walked over to his car and felt quite happy with himself. He drove home and slept well that night.

CHAPTER FIVE

DAY THREE

Amery arrived back at the unit at seven am. He wasn't the first. Peter was already there and marking frantically on the white board. He turned as Amery walked in and said, "Mornin', guv!" to which Amery replied, "Great, Peter! I see you have been busy. Now how is that time-line working out?"

"From what I can see, there are some gaps in time - so!" Peter paused, then continued "The following need to be looked at and probably interviewed. Albanus needs interviewing. He needs to account for his actions between eleven-fifteen and one-fifty, when he was in the park. His vehicle and clothing should be looked at too. It wasn't clear if he was carrying anything when he returned to the car in the parking lot."

"Next, Palmer and Tamarind. They were in the park between twelve forty-five and one fifty-nine, so they need to be interviewed, and we need to look at Palmer's car. Palmer arrived back at the gym at two fifteen and there was nothing, other than clothing in his locker."

"The guy that found the kid, Cooper, was interviewed by PC Johnson at the scene, but you might want to give him another look, too." He looked at Amery, who was studying the white board.

"Any news on fresh forensics or DNA?" Amery asked, though he knew that DNA testing could take ten days to two weeks.

"Nothing yet, guv, but it's a bit early in the morning." he replied, as the door opened and Merriweather entered the unit, carrying three cardboard cups of coffee.

"Morning, all!" he called out as he stepped inside, closing the door behind him and juggling with the coffees, so as not to drop them. He put them down on the table, handing one to Thomas and one to Amery, saying, "I see we made progress." He looked at the white board and DC Thomas. "Where shall we start this morning, guv'nor?" he asked, as he lifted the lid on his coffee and took a sip.

"Thanks for the coffee!" said Amery. "We need to interview this Howard Albanus, and Jonathan Palmer. I want you" - he looked at Thomas - "to get me more information on Samuel Tamarind. I need to know how old he is, first, and where he lives. We will probably interview him later. I'm not too worried about the Cindy girl or those other young men as I think we have accounted for them on the CCTV from the mall."

He too lifted the lid on the coffee and drank some of it. "We might go and check on Cooper, who found the girl, but we can do that later." He thought for a moment, then continued "With what we have here, I think I'll get a couple of warrants. I'll give the Chief Constable a call to arrange it before we go visit Albanus and Palmer."

Corinna arrived at eight forty-five, said good morning, and immediately set about typing up the statements that were left in her inbox next to her computer.

An envelope arrived, addressed to Amery. On opening it, he found it contained photographs of the victim and crime scene, together with various reports including footprints, pawprints and fingerprints, but no DNA yet. Unfortunately, there were no matches to the prints on record. After Amery had studied the reports, he passed them on for Thomas and Merriweather to read.

Corinna passed her typed sheets to Thomas, who examined them and collated them with his other documents. Then she said to him, "I've arranged for a kettle and some mugs to be brought over this morning, and I have brought some coffee and sugar in, and later I'll nip out and get some milk, If it's OK with you, Pete?"

"That's great, Corinna, thank you! We'll need that later on today, I'm sure." replied Thomas.

The phone on Amery's desk rang and he picked it up.

"DI Amery?" he said, then "Yes. Yes. OK.

Thank you."

Then he put the phone down. Having gone over the documents over and over again, Amery stood up, stretched his back out, picked up his pen and put it in the breast pocket of his jacket, turned to Merriweather and said, "OK, Merry, let's get this show on the road!" then continued "We've got to go to the station, the warrants are ready. Pick them up, get a few uniform guys, and brief them before they come with us. Then, first stop will be Howard Albanus. OK! Let's go!" he repeated, walking across to the door and outside, followed by Merriweather.

Having made the call earlier, there were six officers ready and waiting. The desk sergeant handed Merriweather the warrants.

"All in order, sir!" he said as he passed the papers over to Amery. "There are six PCs here and two cars. If you want a van, I can arrange it."

"No." replied Amery. "Two cars will be fine. Are these boys experienced?" he asked.

"Four of them have a lot of experience but the other two have only been in the job for eighteen months. They'll follow instructions and procedures, so you shouldn't have any problems."

"Thank you." said Amery, as he walked toward the six uniforms waiting in the side room.

"OK, gentlemen," started Amery "there are two separate warrants we have to execute today. I don't want any mistakes, or any evidence compromised, so listen carefully and follow my instructions to the letter! Is that clear?" The assembled group of police officers nodded.

"Our first target is a young man named Howard Albanus. He lives with his mother at twenty-seven Fortune Gate Lane, and we will not, I repeat not, use blue lights when approaching the house. He owns a black Escort, registration number N121 HOW. We need the car untouched, so that Forensics can go over it. We may have to get it moved back here to be examined or taken away, but either way I don't want any of your grubby hands on it."

"Next, I need to have him brought here for interview. If necessary I will arrest him, but I am hoping he will come in to help us with our enquiries! However, he is only seventeen years of age, and therefore we will need a responsible adult present during the interview. His mother might accompany him, but in case she doesn't, I want someone here."

"Thirdly, we need to go through the property and any outhouses with a fine-toothed comb. We are looking for the clothing he wore on Monday. A pair of dark blue denim jeans and a blue jumper, and the missing clothing of the victim. But also you must look for photographs, letters, anything that might connect him to the girl. I understand he knows a lot about computers, so if you find one or more computers, we need to secure them. I only want the guys who have done this before to be involved in the search. I understand that there are four of you who are experienced at this. The other two of you can watch the property and his car."

"We are looking for anything that can connect Albanus with Sofia Archer, the murdered young woman. We are particularly looking for the items of clothing belonging to Sofia that were not found at the scene of the crime. I need to confirm his movements between eleven-fifteen am and one-fifty pm last Monday, which I can do in interview, I hope. Make sure you wear proper gloves, and if you find anything I want it bagged and tagged, and I want you to shout and to stop immediately! If we find anything, I want forensics to continue the search. Those of you who've done this before, you will know the routine and procedures. We can't afford to make any mistakes. The rest of you can secure the premises, bring Albanus here, lock him up prior to interview, and ensure that he does not talk to anyone."

"We will execute the second warrant after I have interviewed Albanus, and this is for Jonathan Palmer. He lives with his parents and sister at Honeypot Lodge, Parkway. I am hoping I don't have to arrest him either, and that he will also attend the police station willingly, to help us with our enquiries."

"We have the warrant to search his premises, and are looking for anything that will connect him to Sofia Archer likewise. He may have a computer, so we will seize that, mobile phones, and anything else. He drives a red Audi. We need to secure that for Forensics, so the two of you who have not done this before can ensure that both the rest of his family, and his car, are secured while the search is taking place. We have some of his clothing from his gym locker, of which he may be unaware, but I want any other clothing that he was wearing on Monday."

"I do not want any cock-up on either of these searches. Is that clear?"

The officers in the room said almost in unison "Yes, sir!"

Amery continued, "While we are interviewing Albanus, when we get back here, you can get some 'grub', but don't go far. I'm hoping this won't take long, and I want to get both these interviews done today!"

They all left the building. Amery and Merriweather got into their unmarked car. Three officers got into each of the other marked cars.

CHAPTER SIX

ALBANUS

It was now eleven am, as Amery gave Merriweather Cooper's address, which he punched into the satnav before driving off towards Fortune Gate Lane. Using radio communication only, they approached number twenty-seven, where they noticed the black Ford Escort parked outside.

Two cars stopped outside the front of the house, while the third car drove around the back of the house to make sure that no one could enter or leave the premises. Amery, Merriweather and two of the police officers walked up to the front door, while the third police officer stood by the Ford Escort. Amery knocked, and the door was opened a few moments later by a woman in her mid-thirties. She was dressed in a blue and red cotton dress, her hair tied in a bun on top of her head. She had furry slippers on her feet and held a cigarette in her right hand.

"Yes?" she said, as she opened the door "Can I

help you?" But her voice trailed off as she noticed the two uniformed police officers standing behind Amery and Merriweather. Amery stepped inside the entrance.

"Mrs. Albanus, I presume?" Amery started, and she nodded. "We have a warrant to inspect these premises, and we would like to talk to Howard Albanus. I believe he is your son." he said, waving the warrant at her. Merriweather held his warrant card up for her to see.

She stood stunned for a moment or two, then turned to the foot of the stairs and called up,

"Howard, there are some people here to see you!"

Amery and Merriweather, followed by the two officers, walked into the hallway just inside the door. They heard a door open and footsteps sounding on wooden floorboards, approaching the staircase. Then a young man appeared. Amery and Merriweather knew him immediately by the blond hair they had seen in the video footage which they had watched the day before. He hesitated at the top of the stairs. Amery immediately said in a soft calm voice,

"OK, lad, we just want to talk to you, so don't think about running away. There are officers all around the house and we just want to talk to you."

Albanus seemed frozen for a moment or two, then looked from left to right, as if he were thinking about running away, but then he turned, looked back towards them, and started to walk down the stairs. As he reached the bottom step, Amery took hold of his arm, and said,

"We need you to accompany us to the police station, Howard, and help us with our enquiries. Are you willing to come with us? I don't want to arrest you. I just need you to answer some questions. Is that alright with you, Mrs. Albanus?" he asked, as he turned to look at her.

"What has he done?" pleaded Mrs. Albanus.

"I'm not saying he's done anything, Mrs. Albanus, but we need to talk to him about what has been going on here lately!"

He was being deliberately vague, but he knew Howard would know what he was talking about, and it wouldn't take a genius to know it was about the murder of Sofia Archer. Howard didn't say a word. He didn't resist. He just went pale, as the blood drained from his face. Merriweather took his arm and led him to the police car outside. He placed Howard's hands behind his back and handcuffed him. The officer who had been standing by Howard's car opened the back door of the police car, and Howard was seated inside.

By radio Merriweather ordered two of the officers who were at the back of the house to start the search in the outbuildings, and the third officer to secure the car at the front of the house. He turned to Howard and said,

"Have you got the keys to your car, Howard?" Howard shook his head. "Where are they, Howard? I'd rather the car was opened with the key, than damage the car, if we have to force an entry." Howard answered,

"In the kitchen, on the key hooks. Mum knows

where they are." His head hanging down, he closed his eyes.

Merriweather put a call into forensics to come and collect the car, saying he would have the keys by the time they got there. Then he went back to the house, while the police constable watched and waited with Howard. Mrs Albanus was standing in the hallway and still looked in shock, so Merriweather said to her,

"Why don't you show me the kitchen? Because Howard said his car keys are in there."

Without speaking, she walked down the hallway and into the room at the end, which was the kitchen. In the middle of the room, three chairs stood around a small wooden table covered with a blue, white, and decidedly dirty tablecloth. Also in the room there was an electric cooker, a washing machine, a butler sink full of dirty dishes, and a wooden draining board. A tea towel hung from a hook below the sink, The room had fitted kitchen units, and a fridge freezer that looked out of place. There was an alcove at the rear, a basket sitting on the floor in the corner of the kitchen, and a door that opened onto the garden. Through a window over the sink, Merriweather could see two of the police officers going through a wooden shed at the end of the garden.

"Now, Howard said the keys to his car were on a hook somewhere here." said Merriweather, looking around the kitchen, then at her.

She pointed to the wall near the back door, and he noticed the hooks with keys hanging on it.

"Why don't you make us a nice cup of tea while they carry on with what they are doing?" Merriweather said, again being deliberately vague and motioning at the ceiling, where he could hear the noise of people moving around.

Of course it was the search in progress.

She took the electric kettle to the sink, filled it with water, placed it on its stand and flicked it on. She opened a cupboard above the kettle and took out two mugs, placing them next to the kettle, and taking a couple of tea bags from a tin in the cupboard, dropped one in each cup. While doing so she muttered,

"I don't understand. I don't understand." Then she turned to Merriweather, "What has Howard done? He's a good boy!"

Merriweather answered, "Well, that's what we are hoping to find out. Let's hope it's nothing. How's that tea coming on?" he endeavoured to change the subject. "I'd like milk, if you've got some?"

She turned to the refrigerator and took out a bottle of milk, pouring a little into each mug on top of the tea bag. Merriweather flinched, but said nothing. She put the bottle back into the fridge just as the kettle boiled. She poured the boiling water into the mugs and handed one to Merriweather. The tea bag floated to the top of the cup.

"Oh!" she said. "Do you want sugar?"

"No, thanks." replied Merriweather. He

continued, "Why don't you sit down?"

Taking her by the arm, he guided her to one of the chairs around the table. Looking around the kitchen again, Merriweather's eyes were drawn to the basket near the back door. He walked over to it and lifted the lid. As expected, it contained dirty laundry.

"How often do you manage to do your washing?" he asked her.

She replied, "About once a week. Why do you ask?"

Merriweather replied, "I need to see the clothes that Howard was wearing the day before yesterday. His dark blue denim jeans and blue jumper."

"I'm sure they are in the basket. I'll get them out for you." she said, as she went to get up from the chair, but Merriweather quickly interrupted, "No, that's fine, you just sit there! If they are in here, I'll sort them out."

He lifted the whole basket and placed it near the door. He heard footsteps on the stairs and in the hallway. Amery opened the door and came into the kitchen. Merriweather looked at him and motioned to the laundry basket.

"I think his clothes are in there."

"OK." said Amery, then he turned to Mrs. Albanus.

Turning to him, with tears welling up in her eyes,

she spoke, "I don't understand! I don't understand! Has Howard done something?"

"Mrs. Albanus, I am sorry about this, but I have people coming here soon to go through your house and some of Howard's things thoroughly, and I think if you visited a friend or family member for a few hours you might be more comfortable. Now do you have any family? Can I phone someone for you?"

He looked at her sitting at the table, with the mug of untouched tea with a tea bag floating on the top, slopping tea onto the dirty tablecloth in front of her. She looked pathetic.

"I could call my aunt, she lives a few streets away, but Howard has the car, oh, I can't get there." she replied.

"Now, Mrs. Albanus, you make the call and I'll make sure that we get you there. I promise we will look after your house like it was our own. Do you give us permission to ask Howard for his DNA and fingerprints, so that we may eliminate him from our enquiries?"

"OK." she said, as she got up from the table.

Merriweather followed her upstairs, where she put on her shoes, collected her handbag and slipped on a jacket.

Amery had called in forensics and they were on their way.

In Howard's bedroom they found a couple of letters from Sofia, a computer and a mobile phone. So they bagged, tagged, dated, and signed the letters and phone, and then they awaited forensics to go through the room thoroughly and get into the computer. Care was taken in every part of the search.

Amery instructed the other officers to stay at the house, one to make sure the car was not touched until forensics arrived. They were to stay outside the house and not let anyone else in until after forensics had finished and the car taken away. Once the house was secured they could then return to the station.

When they arrived, forensics examined the laundry basket from the kitchen. The dark blue denim jeans, jumper, underwear and other items of men's clothing were removed for further examination. Three of the officers had by now returned to the police station with Howard, who was now in custody, but not arrested, as he was helping with enquiries.

Merriweather and Amery drove Mrs. Albanus to her aunt's house a few streets away, where they left her.

Merriweather and Amery returned to the police station. PC Johnson was there, and offered them a coffee, which they graciously accepted and drank, before they started the interview with Howard.

"Do we have a responsible adult who can sit in for this interview?" Amery asked Johnson. "Yes." replied Johnson "Her name is Kathy Green. She's on the list of approved adults."

"He hasn't been charged, has he?" Johnson asked.

"Not yet, but we need everything clean as a whistle, transparent, and above board." said Amery. "So, let's get him up!"

Amery and Merriweather went into the interview room and Merriweather placed the tape into the machine. Johnson brought Howard in and sat him down at the table. They were introduced to Kathy Green, who had followed them in. Merriweather switched the recorder on and said,

"Twenty-ninth July 1998, one thirty pm, Newpark Police Station. Interview with Howard Albus, aged seventeen years, date of birth twenty-fourth August, nineteen eighty. Present, Detective Sergeant Merriweather."

Amery said "Detective Inspector Amery."

Kathy Green said, "Responsible person Kathy Green, aged over twenty-five years."

"So, Howard, how are you?" asked Amery.

"OK." said Howard.

"Can you confirm your date of birth for me, Howard?" said Amery.

Howard replied "Twenty-fourth of August, nineteen-eighty."

"Do you know why you are here?" asked Amery.

"I think so." replied Howard.

"And why is that?" asked Amery.

"It's because of Sofia, isn't it?" said Howard.

"That's right!" said Amery. "I want to try to eliminate you from my enquiries. Your mother said you would give us a DNA sample and your fingerprints. Are you alright with that, Howard?"

Howard replied "Of course I am."

Merriweather immediately took the DNA kit from behind him and took samples from Howard's mouth. He also took fingerprints and safely stored them, placing them back on the table behind him.

"What can you tell me about Sofia?" Amery continued.

"I loved her." said Howard. "She was my girlfriend."

Amery was surprised by that response, but did not show it. "How often did you see her, if she was your girlfriend?" he asked.

"We couldn't meet as often as we wanted. It was difficult when we were in school. Too many prying eyes, and no privacy, so we used to email each other and send pictures."

"So how long have you been sending pictures to each other?" Amery asked.

"About four months." was the reply.

"Do you keep them on your computer? Or do you print them off?" Amery asked.

"I keep them on my computer." Howard replied.

Amery and Merriweather knew that if there were any emails or photographs on his computer, forensics would find them, so he didn't pursue that any further for the time being.

"And did you write to each other in letters?" asked Amery, knowing that they had found some letters from Sofia to Howard in his room.

"She has written me a couple of letters. She put them in my locker at school. I have them in my room at home." he answered, confirming what Amery already knew.

"You arranged to meet her on Monday, didn't you?" Amery asked him

"Yes." Howard replied.

"Why did you keep it a secret?"

"Because her friends don't think I'm good enough for her, but she loved me, and we just wanted to be together. She told me in her messages and emails that she loved me. She arranged to meet me. She wrote me letters and sent photographs, lots of photographs." He began to cry "I'm sorry, so sorry. I loved her."

Merriweather asked him, "So, Howard, tell us what happened on Monday?"

He wiped his nose on his sleeve and started to talk:

"We arranged to meet in the park. You know the country park. We thought it would be private and no one would see us. It wasn't like it was a week-end or anything, so we didn't expect there to be anyone around."

"We arranged to meet at half past eleven, so I went to the Mall and left about quarter past eleven, then went across to the park and waited where no one could see me from the road or the Mall.

Sofia came over at about half past eleven, and we held hands and walked further into the park. We walked for about fifteen minutes, then sat down under some trees and talked. I don't know what we talked about, but we just talked and then we kissed each other." He stopped and sobbed a bit more.

"Why are you crying?" Merriweather asked.

"Because I touched her breast and she pushed me away. Said she didn't want me to touch her there. I said I was sorry, and we kissed again. We must have been there for at least an hour, and we were lying on the ground now, and I wanted to touch her all over, but she still said no, so we just kissed and kissed, then I tried to touch her again, but she shouted at me to stop, so I did." He paused again for a few seconds and Merriweather asked,

"Do you know what time it was then?"

"It must have been about one o'clock by then, so

I told her it would be best if I just went home, and she said she would go for a walk before going back to the Mall, so no one would see us together, and she would send me a message later, and I got up, and we kissed again before I walked back to the Mall."

"Where did Sofia go?" asked Amery.

"She just walked off in the opposite direction."

"So, what did you do then?" Amery asked him again.

"I was walking back to the mall when I heard noises. Moans and grunting noises! I thought something was wrong with a dog or something. I feel so ashamed and I'm so sorry!" he said.

"Don't worry Howard, just tell us what happened." Merriweather said with some compassion.

"I stopped and got onto my hands and knees and crept forward trying to see what the noises were and trying to keep quiet; and then I saw them. The two of them were half naked and he was doing things men shouldn't do. I thought it was disgusting, but I couldn't help looking. It made me hard."

He looked up at Amery for a minute then said, "You know what I mean?" He looked at Kathy and turned back and turned his eyes back onto the table. "And I . . ." - he paused – "then . . ." - he paused again - "I played with myself!" He stopped. He was breathing in short breaths.

Amery, Meriweather and Kathy Green showed no emotion or disgust. Amery thought to himself, "Was this voyeurism? The Sex Offenders Act of nineteen ninety-seven repealed almost all of the Sexual Offences Act of nineteen fifty-six, but was there intent?"

"No! It seemed there was no intent, just stupidity!" so he decided to let it go for now.

Howard continued, "I watched them and watched them for ages. They went on and on and on and then they were cuddling and kissing, and I watched until they finished what they were doing, and when they lay on the ground looking up at the sky, and I could hear them breathing heavily and panting like animals, I crept away."

"They disgusted me, and I felt violated, myself! I felt terrible. When I got near the edge of the park, I straightened myself up, and I remember holding my arms around my jumper, or in front of me, because I didn't want anyone to see the stain in my pants."

"I'm sorry, so sorry! I shouldn't have watched them! I know it was wrong, but I couldn't help myself! I crossed the road and got in my car and went home."

"Do you know who they were?" Amery asked him.

"It was Samuel and Jonathan Palmer." he answered.

Both Amery and Merriweather looked at one another with knowing looks. At least the entry and exit to the park matched what they already knew from the CCTV, and now they knew that Tamarind and Palmer were together between those times.

"So, Howard, are you telling us that you didn't see Sofia after about one o'clock?" Amery asked.

"Yes." he replied.

"Did you see anyone else at any time you were in the park, when you with Sofia, or watching the other boys, or at any time at all?"

"There was a collie dog sniffing around, and a man whistled, and the dog went to him. That was while I was . . . " He paused. Then he continued "watching, and I don't remember anyone else."

"OK, Howard, that will be all for now, but we want you to stay with us a little longer. I'll arrange for you to get a drink and a sandwich if you would like that?" said Amery.

"OK." said Howard.

"Interview ended two thirty pm." Merriweather said as he clicked the machine down. Then he took the tape out of the machine, marked it up with the time, and signed it, before holding it in his hand.

"Now Howard," said Amery "you go with DS Merriweather and he will get you settled somewhere and get you that sandwich. Then we will arrange to get you home a little later."

He smiled at him and Howard, Kathy and Merriweather got up and left the interview room. Merriweather saw Johnson and spoke to him, "Can you arrange for some grub and a drink for the kid, and keep him safe till we get back, then get this" - handing Johnson the tape he had just taken from the machine - "over to the unit for DC Thomas, and send this DNA stuff to forensics?"

"Of course! I'll do it straight away!" Johnson said, taking the tape and putting the bag of DNA evidence and prints into his pocket, then he led Howard by the arm into another room. Kathy said goodbye, and left the building.

Merriweather returned to Amery and put in a call to Thomas to say the tape was on its way, the DNA would be going to forensics, and they were now going to Palmer's home.

CHAPTER SEVEN

JONATHAN PALMER

Regrouping, the officers drove off and arrived at
Honeypot Lodge at three pm. Using the intercom on the
gate, they announced themselves.

"Good afternoon. It's DI Amery and DS
Merriweather again. I have a few more questions. Can
you open the gate please?"

With a buzz and click, the gates started to open.
As Merriweather drove in, the other two police cars
followed closely behind, and the gates closed behind them.
Approaching the house, they could see the Red Audi on
the gravel drive. Using the radio communication in the
car, Amery instructed one of the officers to make sure that
no-one drove the car away. If the keys were in the
ignition, he was to take them out and hold onto them.
Other than that, he was to do nothing with the car.

They parked the three vehicles as the door to the

house opened. Amery and Merriweather walked towards Mr. Palmer, who was standing in the entrance.

"Please come in" said Mr. Palmer, surprised when four burly uniformed police officers followed them in. Another officer stood by the door and held it open. Mr. Palmer showed them into the drawing room again, offered them tea or coffee and asked how he could help.

"We would like to speak to your son, Mr. Palmer. Is he here?" Amery asked.

Two officers were standing inside the drawing room with Amery and Merriweather. The other two stood in the hallway outside the drawing room, ensuring that the door was kept open.

"Yes." said Mr. Palmer, looking very puzzled and a little concerned "I'll call him." And with that he shuffled past the two officers and called to his son "Jonathan! Jonathan, please come down here immediately!" Then looked back at Amery, who gave him a little smile to put him at ease. They heard movement, at the top of the stairs on the landing, then footsteps coming down. Jonathan Palmer appeared at the doorway to the drawing room.Amery spoke first:

"Thank you, Jonathan, for coming so quickly. You were very helpful last time we met, and I was wondering if you wouldn't mind helping us with our enquiries a little more." Jonathan beamed at the men in the room.

"Of course sir, I'll help in anyway, I can."

"It would be helpful if you would come to the station and answer some questions." Amery said.

Jonathan hesitated for a moment or two, then replied,

"I don't mind that. I've never been to a police station before. It should prove very interesting."

Amery cringed and thought to himself, "Cocky little bastard!" but actually said "Thank you, that would be very helpful."

He walked over to Jonathan and led him outside to one of the police cars. He opened the rear door, swiftly took his handcuffs from his pocket and locked them over Jonathan's wrists, having pulled his arms behind his back, and told him to get in the back seat. It was done so quickly that Jonathan hardly knew what had happened, and went to say something, but Amery shut the car door saying, "Thank you for your help! I'll follow on shortly."

Then he instructed one of the officers to drive him to the station, whispering, "Lock him up, he's helping us with our enquiries! Afterwards, come back here. You will be needed to get the other guys back."

As the officer drove off down the drive, Amery went back into the house and asked Palmer Senior to open the gates to let the car out, telling him that he would be following on shortly. Palmer opened the gates for the car to leave.

It was at this point that Amery showed Palmer

Senior the warrant to search the premises and the car. Palmer was taken aback, as he had not expected this. Mrs. Palmer had by now joined them in the drawing room. Juliette eventually appeared at the top of the staircase, and Merriweather asked her to join them in the drawing room.

The family seated themselves, occupying various chairs. No one spoke. They just looked at each other in amazement, not believing what was happening.

"We want to start in Jonathan's room, Mr Palmer." Amery began "Which room is it, please?"

Palmer told him it was at the top of the stairs, second on the left. Merriweather and two of the uniforms climbed the stairs.

"We do appreciate your co-operation!" Amery smiled at the family, continuing "I'll leave this officer with you while I help them upstairs!"

Mr. Palmer was so dumbfounded he did not speak, just nodded, and Amery went upstairs while one of the officers walked into the drawing room and closed the door behind him.

They were looking for anything that connected Jonathan to Sofia, and they wanted to find his chinos, jumper, and the sneakers he wore to and from the gym.

After a thorough search of the house the only thing they could find were the sneakers, which they bagged and tagged. They were not the Gucci trainers he wore the first day they met him. They were the same ones he had on at the gym, and they had mud in the grooves in their soles. There seemed to be nothing else of any consequence. No letters or photographs connecting Jonathan to Sofia.

They found his mobile phone, which was also bagged and tagged. Then, on the inside of his wardrobe door, they discovered a calendar marked with red crosses on various days of the week - including the Monday which actually had two red crosses. "What did that mean?" they both wondered.

So they took it, bagged it, and tagged it. Afterwards Amery radioed for forensic to take the car away and they returned to the drawing room. He told three of the officers they could leave, and take the evidence back to the station.

"Mr. Palmer," started Amery "thank you for your co-operation. It was good of Jonathan to help us with our enquiries, and I will try to be as quick as I can. I don't seem able to find a pair of chinos and the jumper that Jonathan was wearing on Monday. Can you shed any light on it?" He looked at Mrs. Palmer.

"They went to the cleaners on Tuesday! We have a collection; early Tuesday mornings and they will be back on Thursday. Is it important? I can call you when they are back."

"Not to worry, Mrs. Palmer." He thought testing would be useless, after cleaning chemicals had been all over them. Then he turned to Palmer Senior, "Thank you again for your help! Jonathan's car will be collected within the hour, and I will leave a couple of officers here until it is."

Palmer was still struggling to understand what had just happened, but he turned to Amery and replied, "We will help in any way we can, Inspector. I'm sure Jonathan didn't have anything to do with anything illegal. I can come and collect him when he is ready, if that helps."

"Thank you again, Mr. Palmer. I'll make sure you are called as soon as he is ready." Amery replied as he turned and left the room. Merriweather and the police officer followed, closing the door behind them, leaving the family in the drawing room.

Once outside the house, Merriweather closed the front door while Amery turned to the two officers and said, "Stay here until forensics arrive. A car should arrive back for you soon but don't leave until forensics have done so first. You know not to get involved in conversations with them, don't you?" he said, pointing back to the house.

Then he and Merriweather got in their car and drove back to the police station. On the way, Amery called Thomas, and asked if he had heard from WPC Scott, and how the family were doing, and if there were any updates from forensics. Thomas reported that Scott was still with the family, that there was still an officer outside their house, that the press had been onto him, but he had given them no information, other than that an investigation was taking place. Nothing further from forensics.

He had a call from HQ and forensics, who had collected Albanus's car, and were now on their way to pick up the Palmer car, and take it to HQ. Amery said he had some stuff that needed forensic examination, but that he was going to use it with the interview with Palmer, before passing it on.

By the time his conversation had ended, Merry was pulling into the police station car park. Amery got out of the car first, Merriweather following with the evidence bags.

On reaching the interview desk, Amery asked to be provided with some coffee and a couple of biscuits for himself and Merriweather, and also a jug of water and paper cups, before they started the interview with Jonathan Palmer. Having had the coffee, they discussed how they were going to handle the interview.

It was agreed that Amery would lead, but that Merriweather would back up if timings were out of sync, and interject where appropriate. Much like they always did! No good boy, bad boy. . . Those days were long gone. Jonathan Palmer was a cocky little blighter who needed bringing back down to earth!

Amery opened the interview room door and called to the desk sergeant to fetch Palmer. Merriweather gathered up the disposable coffee cups and threw them in the bin. He put a tape into the machine. He put the evidence bags on the small table behind him with the DNA and fingerprint equipment he needed and finally he put out a jug and water and paper cups.

Palmer was brought in.

Amery said to the custody officer, "You don't need those cuffs on him. He is here, helping us with our enquiries. He's not a prisoner!" All very sardonically. He turned to Jonathan and said "Jonathan, sit down and let's talk!"

Merriweather turned the tape on and said, "Twenty-ninth July, nineteen ninety-eight, at Newpark Police Station, interview with Jonathan Andrew Palmer, twenty-ninth July, nineteen ninety-eight, at seventeen oh four hours, present Detective Sergeant Merriweather."

Amery said, "and Detective Inspector Amery."

Jonathan did not look happy, saying, "I really don't understand why I'm being treated like this! Am I under arrest? I offered to come here willingly to help you, because I know nothing about Sofia other than what I told you yesterday, and you put me in handcuffs and throw me into a cell!"

"Really sorry about all that, Jonathan, but now you're here let's talk! Would you willingly provide me with DNA and your fingerprints, so we can exclude you from our enquiries?" Amery asked.

Jonathan said he was more than willing. Then, while Merriweather took mouth swabs and fingerprints, which he carefully secured and bagged up, Amery said,

"You told me yesterday that you spent the Monday at the gym." and looked intently at Jonathan.

"Well? So?" retorted Jonathan, "What else do you want to know?"

"Well?" said Amery "and So?" he was mimicking him. "It would appear that you did NOT" - he emphasised the not - "spend all day at the gym, so let's talk seriously. You will tell me exactly where you went, what you did and whom you met!" Amery was in deadly earnest.

Merriweather took the evidence bags, with the pair of trainers, calendar and phone, from the table behind, and placed them on the table in front of him, so that Jonathan could see them.

"Oh!" Jonathan was shocked. "Well I did leave the gym for a while, but I did not see Sofia, really I didn't!" He was panicking, and it showed in his voice.

"Well, Jonathan, we know you left the gym and HOW." - emphasising the how - "But I want you to tell me all about that!" Amery looked at Jonathan, and waited.

Jonathan said nothing. He was obviously thinking about just what to say. Merriweather said, "Come on Jonathan, just relax and let's have the truth this time!"

"OK." said Jonathan "I did the leave the gym. I've done it before and it's a bit of an adventure." He was very nervous. "I open the door to the pool plant equipment, which is at the end of the gents' cubicles and shut it behind me, then go down the corridor and out through the fire door, which I leave a little bit open so I can get back in."

"I found a key in the door once, and couldn't help going to have a look, and realised I could get outside without anyone knowing, so I got a duplicate cut and I've used it ever since. I make sure the fire door to the outside isn't quite closed, so I can get back in later. I've done it loads of times before, so didn't think much of it. In case my father questions where I've been, the computers at the gym will show the time I swipe in and out."

Neither Amery or Merriweather spoke. They just continued to look at Jonathan and waited for him to continue.

"I'd arranged to meet a friend," he said "so I drove to the mall, and . . ." he paused, then continued, "Yes I did go in. I know I said before that I didn't go in, but I was only there for a couple of minutes then I came out, so I didn't really go in!"

He looked at Amery "Did I?" and continued again, "My friend came out, and we sat in my car and talked for a while, then I drove us around town for a bit, and then we went back and parked in the mall car park, and went for a walk in the park, before I went back to the gym!"

He stopped talking and looked down at the table. Merriweather, after waiting a few moments, then asked, "Who did you meet, Jonathan?" and waited for a reply.

"I met my friend." Jonathan replied.

"What's his name Jonathan?" Merriweather was a bit firmer with his question this time.

"Samuel Tamarind." was the eventual reply.

"And how old is Samuel?" Merriweather continued.

"He's seventeen or eighteen, I think." Jonathan replied.

"Why be so secretive about a meeting with a friend Jonathan?" Amery asked.

"I don't know." said Jonathan. "I guess it made it exciting."

"So, when you met him, after a while you went for a walk in the park, you said? What did you do in the park?" Merriweather asked.

Jonathan went pale and licked his lips as his mouth dried up, and he said,

"Can I have a glass of water, please?" Merriweather poured water into a paper cup and passed it to him. Jonathan took the water and drank it all before putting the paper cup on the table.

Merriweather then asked him again, "What did you do in the park, Jonathan?"

Jonathan stared silently into the empty cup. Then he said in a very low voice, "Samuel and I made out."

He didn't look up. He just kept looking into the empty cup. He was a different man now, from the cocky arrogant young man who had met them on the previous

Tuesday morning outside his house.

Amery spoke: "Jonathan, you and Samuel are two consenting adults, so what you do is up to you. But the park isn't the best place, and you might be committing an offence if people see you. Did you know that?' he asked.

"No. I didn't, but we thought it was private. We hid under some bushes in a sort of secluded spot. Please don't tell my parents!" he pleaded.

"Jonathan, there is no reason why I should tell your parents anything. You are an adult, but you know we are investigating the murder of a young woman. You knew her AND you were in the vicinity of the place she was murdered, so you need to tell me the truth, and all of it! Do you understand?" said Amery. He was very serious now.

"Yes, I do, and I'm really sorry about it, but honestly, everything I told you at my house about knowing her is true. I didn't see her on Monday. I really didn't!" he said.

"Who did you see?" Amery asked. "Think hard, because I want to know everyone you saw."

"We passed a man and woman walking a black Labrador dog, when we first went in. I can't say exactly where we saw them, but they were walking around the path and not heading for the Mall, so they didn't exactly pass us, and I don't think I'd recognise them again anyway."

"I could hear some other people talking, and hear breaking branches, but I didn't see them, and then their voices and the sounds faded away. I saw a man with a walking stick. He was walking a small black and white dog, and he was going around the path too, but we didn't get close to him and he wasn't going towards the Mall or car park either. I don't remember anyone else."

"Samuel and I were looking for somewhere out of the way, and found a spot that was quite hidden away under bushes, like private and secluded. I didn't see anyone else, and I didn't see anyone when we were leaving the park either. Samuel went back into the Mall and I drove off back to the gym."

"OK." said Amery. "We'll leave it here for the time being. I just need you to wait here for a little while longer. You can either wait back in the cells, or you can give me your word, and sit outside in the charge of the desk sergeant. He'll get you a cup of coffee, but I need you to wait!

Do you understand? Do you have Samuel's contact details?" Jonathan nodded on both counts and gave Amery and Merriweather Samuel's address.

Merriweather said: "Interview ended eighteen ten." and ejected the tape from the machine, wrote on it and put it into his pocket.

Amery opened the door of the interview room and guided Jonathan Palmer to a seat outside. then he spoke with the desk sergeant, who looked across at Jonathan, smiled and queried, "Milk, sugar?" to which

Jonathan meekly replied, "Yes, please." and patiently set to waiting.

Merriweather passed the DNA evidence to the desk sergeant, asking him to 'get it to forensics PDQ'. He said he would take the tape to the unit himself, later.

CHAPTER EIGHT

SAMUEL TAMARIND

Amery and Merriweather left the police station. Once again Merriweather drove, and they headed out towards the mobile unit.

Amery wanted Merry to hand the tape to Corinna, so she could get it typed up and Thomas could collate the information. Once that was done they drove to the home of Samuel Tamarind, No. 16, Kingsgate Road, which was in the same part of town as the home of Howard Albanus, but several streets away.

Arriving outside number sixteen at around six fifty pm, Merriweather parked the car in the street. There was a group of women standing and talking about twenty metres away from them, and a few young children laughing and shouting to each other, riding bicycles on the pavement.

As they got out of the car, the women looked over towards them and, talking amongst each other, watched them approach the front door of number sixteen. Merriweather gave three loud knocks on the door and waited. The door was opened within a few moments by a tall olive-skinned young man.

"Samuel Tamarind?" asked Amery, and the young man nodded. Showing his warrant card, Amery said,

"I'm DI Amery and this is DS Merriweather." Merry also held up his warrant card. "Can we come in and talk to you?"

"Yes, come in." was the reply. "I'm afraid my parents aren't home from work yet, and my brothers aren't in either, but come in." he repeated, as he led them in. The room opened up into a large living and dining space. "Do you want me?" he asked.

"We do, Samuel. We need to ask you where you were this Monday." Amery replied.

Samuel changed from a handsome olive-skinned young man to a pale, even grey, very sad boy.

"Oh my God!" he cried. "Did someone see me? Oh my God! Has Jonathan said something? Oh my God!" he repeated, as he sank down into an armchair, held his face in his hands, and placed his elbows on his knees.

Amery sat down in a chair opposite him. Merriweather stood behind.

"It's OK, Samuel." soothed Merriweather. "We just need to ask you a few questions." Then he took out his pocketbook and pen, ready to make notes.

Amery spoke. "How old are you, Samuel?" He needed to make sure the boy was old enough to answer questions without his parents being present. Samuel dropped his hands to his knees, looked up at the policemen and replied, "I'm eighteen."

Both Amery and Merriweather breathed a sigh of relief. They could continue with the interview.

"Do you know Sofia Archer?" Amery asked.

Samuel replied, "Sort of. She was at the same school as me and I see her around town sometimes. I might wave at her or occasionally say hello, but I'm not really a friend."

"Did you see her on Monday?" Amery continued.

"I think I saw her at the mall when I was walking around. I think she was with Juliette Palmer, but I didn't take much notice."

"Now Samuel, you left the mall at just after eleven-thirty, didn't you?" Amery told him, and waited for him to answer. Samuel put his hands back over his face, rubbing his forehead with his fingers then replied,

"Yes, sir."

"It's OK, Samuel" said Amery "I only want to confirm where you were, and who you saw. Do you understand?" Samuel kept his face in his hands and replied again,

"Yes, sir."

"So, who did you meet, Samuel?" Amery asked.

Samuel dropped his hands again and stared at Amery and Merriweather and, raising his voice, wailed, "You know who I met! You know who! It was Jonathan Palmer, and we went for a drive and a walk in the park!"

"Good." said Amery. "That's what Jonathan told us. Now, who did you see in the park?"

Samuel looking confused, and asked "Who?"

"Yes." said Amery, "Who else did you see in the park?"

"I was with Jonathan, and I think I saw a couple of people walking dogs, and I know we heard other people but didn't see them, then we didn't hear anyone else. We were on our own and I don't think anyone saw us. We were there for about an hour, I think, but I didn't talk to anyone else." Samuel looked from Amery to Merriweather, then in a low voice said "Jonathan told you this, didn't he?"

Amery looked at him and replied, "Yes, he told us, Samuel, but I want you to tell me if you recognised any of the people you saw in the park. Those walking their dogs!"

Samuel, raising his hand to his forehead again, replied, "No! I didn't recognise any of them! The couple I saw first had a black Labrador dog, and the second man we saw had a walking stick and a black and white collie dog. But I didn't see any of their faces. They were walking the other way, away from us."

Amery spoke to him again as he got up from the chair, "Thank you for your help, Samuel! If we need anything else, we'll come and see you again, but before I go, would you be willing to give us a DNA sample, and your fingerprints, so we can eliminate you from our enquiries?" Samuel, looking like he didn't really understand, said, "Yes, of course."

Merriweather broke open the sterilized DNA kit he had in his pocket, asked Samuel to open his mouth, took a sample, and sealed it in a sterilized bag. He couldn't take fingerprints there, but he knew he could get Samuel to come to the station later, if they became necessary.

Amery turned towards Merriweather, and they went outside and back into their car.

The group of women were still gathered and looking across at them, as they drove off and headed back to the unit. Amery telephoned Jonathan Palmer's father on the way, telling him he could go to the police station and pick his son up. He also telephoned the station and told the desk sergeant to release Albanus and to take him to his mother, who was with an aunt a couple of streets away from their house. And if forensics had finished at their house, the sergeant should offer to take him and his mother back to their home.

They arrived back at the unit at eight pm. Thomas and Corinna had gone. Merriweather put Samuel's DNA sample in the small fridge and left a note for Thomas to get it to forensics in the morning. Amery said, "Nothing else we can do tonight, Merry! It's too late, and I need food, so let's call it quits. If you fancy a pint, we can drop in the Wild Buck and talk."

Merriweather looked at him, grinned and said, "Have you ever heard me refuse a pint, guv'nor? I'm pretty hungry myself. It's been a long day!"

Amery got into his own car and they drove off to the Wild Buck, which was about eight miles away. They arrived around eight thirty pm, parked up, and walked inside. The pub wasn't very busy. There was nobody at the bar, and just a half dozen tables with people eating. Grabbing a menu, they headed for the bar, ordered a couple of pints of ale, fish and chips, then they found a table and sat down.

Amery was first to speak, "We've got a lot to look at tomorrow, Merry, and this case gets more confusing by the hour!"

"You're right, guv. I'm hoping Thomas can piece together the evidence we have, and that we get more forensic reports in the morning, but for now I need food!" he exclaimed.

Amery nodded, recalling the previous evening when he was sitting in a pub, eating and drinking with a beautiful young woman. Should he call her when he got home? He looked at his watch, which showed eight forty-five pm. No! He thought he'd leave it a while and see how he felt tomorrow. Anyway, it would probably be past ten pm when he got home, and he did have another early start in the morning.

He and Merry chatted about the weather, holidays and family; drank their pint, ate their fish and chips, had another pint, then drove to their respective homes.

CHAPTER NINE

MORNING OF DAY FOUR

Amery woke at five thirty am. He hadn't slept well, too much going round in his head. It looked like the suspects were no longer suspects, but the forensics hadn't come back yet, so anyone could be lying to him. But he doubted it. His years of experience told him that the boys, or young men, he and Merry had interviewed, were telling the truth.

He rolled out of bed and went down to the kitchen to make himself a fresh brew of cafetière coffee. He filled the kettle with water from the tap, put the kettle on to boil, and took the packet of coffee out of the cupboard. Then he put two large scoops into the cafetière sitting on the side. He looked in the refrigerator for milk or cream, but the fridge was virtually empty. Two eggs sat in the egg-rack on the door, half a bottle of wine, which he took out and emptied down the sink.

He spied a lump of orange cheese called Red

Leicester. He wondered why they called orange cheese 'red'? "Very strange!" he thought to himself. Closing the 'fridge, he decided black coffee would hit the spot anyway.

When the kettle boiled, he switched the gas off, poured the water into the jug and sat the plunger on the top. Leaving the jug of coffee on the side to 'brew', he went back upstairs into the bathroom, turned the basin taps on, took out his razor and shaving foam from the bathroom cupboard above it, and shaved.

He stripped off, turned the shower on, and stepped in. The hot water running down his body gave him a refreshing burst of energy, and taking the shower gel, he washed his hair, and then his body, from top to bottom.

He was six feet two inches tall, slim built, but solid. His muscles weren't bulging but he had a six pack that many men his age wished they still had. He wasn't particularly hairy. He knew a lot of women liked hairy men, but there wasn't anything he could do about that. A few chest hairs, and more where they were meant to be. Anyway, he wasn't really interested in women, though Julia still passed through his mind.

Turning the shower off, he stepped out and grabbed a towel. He first rubbed his hair with it, then wrapped it round his waist. Barefoot, he walked back downstairs into the kitchen. He pushed the plunger on the cafetière down, took a mug from the rack and poured himself a coffee. He looked at the clock on the cooker. It registered six am. By six thirty he had finished the whole of the cafetière, washed up his mug and the empty jug. He dressed, cleaned his teeth, tidied the bathroom up, threw back the covers on his bed, and drove back to the unit.

He arrived at almost the same time as Merriweather, at around seven am. There was already another car outside. It was Thomas, who was busily collating the information from the previous day. He had seen the DNA sample that had been left the night before, and was waiting for a courier to pick it up. Amery and Merriweather sat down, looking at the white board filled with information.

There were forensic reports on Amery's desk, which had been rushed through, but they had still been thorough. The mud on Jonathan's trainers was from the park (but he already knew that!) and the footprints from his trainers did not match those found near Sofia's body.

Corinna arrived at eight am, and immediately started to type and transcribe from the taped interviews, while Thomas, Merriweather and Amery discussed the case, and went over and over the evidence and information they had. By nine am, Corinna asked if they would like coffee, to which the three of them said yes. She made the coffee and passed it to them, also making one for herself. She passed Thomas the latest transcript she had typed up, then sat back at her desk, drinking her coffee.

A police courier arrived, and Corinna gave him the package for forensics, collecting a large envelope from forensics, which she passed to Thomas. He opened the envelope, and spread the information out of the desk in front of Amery and Merriweather.

Amery looked up at the white board and timeline, with the names of those they had interviewed, and those with whom they could confirm their whereabouts, then turned his attention to the reports laid before him. He picked up the first one, read it, then the second, and third, and so on, until he had finished reading them all. Merriweather followed suit and finished reading the last one just after Amery. He picked up the file containing the photos of the crime scene. He had seen many such photos before, but it always hit a spot in his heart when he saw a child.

Sofia wasn't quite a child, but she really wasn't a woman either. Examining the photos, he passed them to Amery, who was also looking at the report from the ME and the report from SOCO. Then Amery picked up one of the photos of the crime scene with his left hand, while holding a report in his right hand, and said,

"Did you notice this, Merry? The footprints at the crime scene are reported as size ten men's walking boots, but that's not the interesting bit. What's interesting is that they are all over the bloody crime scene!" Turning to Thomas he said,

"Pete, can we get this projected larger?"

Thomas replied, " 'Course, guv'nor!"

He took the photo from Amery, walked across to Corinna, and asked her to scan the photo and project it onto the screen above her head. There was a large while screen on the wall of the unit, built in especially for such occasions. Lifting the lid on the scanner, she placed the photo on the glass, closed the lid, and returned to her computer, where she scanned the picture and projected it as requested.

Amery, Merriweather and Thomas stood in front of the projected photograph, concentrating and examining it intently. Then Amery said,

"How could we have missed that? I'm not sure, but I think those size tens belong to Cooper, and if I'm right, why are they everywhere? Look, there are even toe impressions in the soil, and the report says they are probably from the same boots!"

"You're right, but we aren't sure if the boots belong to Cooper!" said Thomas.

"No." said Amery. "But we will bloody well find out soon!" Then he continued "Merry, have we got an address for him?"

"Yes, guv. Got it from Johnson."

"OK, Let's get a search warrant organised and go visit him. Better get Johnson to come with us." said Amery.

While Merriweather made some phone calls to organise the warrant, Corinna asked Thomas if they would like some coffee. He looked at her and asked if she was feeling alright as she had gone a little pale.

"I'm sorry." she said quietly. "I have dealt with murders before and typed up loads of reports, but I've never actually seen the photographs, and that picture sort of shocked me. She was only a child, really, wasn't she? I'm only twenty-seven, but she looks like a baby! It made me feel awful. I'm sorry."

"I understand." said Thomas. "Would you like me to make the coffee?"

"No, that's alright, I'll do it. I need to keep busy and put the image out of my mind."

It was now well past eleven am.

"Good idea!" he told her.

She put the kettle on to boil while filling each mug with a spoonful of coffee and sugar. When the kettle boiled, she filled each mug, then added milk and passed them on to Thomas, not realising that neither Amery nor Merriweather took sugar. Taking the coffee, Amery lifted it to his mouth and sipped a little. He then turned to Merriweather and asked if his coffee had sugar too. Merriweather responded, "Afraid so!"

Thomas overheard and came over to them. "Sorry, guv'nor, the lass was a little upset about the pictures, and she forgot or didn't know. I'll make another."

They looked across at Corinna sitting at her desk with her coffee mug clasped between two hands. She was looking down at her computer.

"Not to worry!" said Amery. "Make a list out for her with who takes what, as I'm sure we will be drinking a lot more coffee before this case is over."

He handed him his mug. Merriweather also passed his mug to him, and Thomas took the two mugs and emptied them. He had to refill the kettle with water before putting it on to boil, but he made two more coffees, without sugar, and handed them to Amery and Merriweather, who no sooner had them than drank them.

By mid-day the warrant was ready. Amery and Merriweather set out for the home of Thomas Cooper. PC Johnson met them outside the house. They didn't take any other back-up this time; for some reason Amery had a feeling he wouldn't need it. He was correct, for when they arrived at Cooper's home there was no reply.

Cooper lived in a semi-detached house in a quiet area of town. Each house had a garage attached and neat and tidy front gardens. Amery asked Johnson about Cooper.

"Do you know, Johnson, you are the only one who has ever seen or spoken to Cooper? I've read the statement from your pocketbook, but none of us has seen him. We have no idea what he looks like! How old do you reckon this Cooper is?"

"I'd say he's fifty, or in his early fifties, Guv. About five foot ten inches. Fairly short dark hair, greying at the sides. He seemed quite genuine, and I followed all the procedures."

Amery was quick to respond. "I'm not saying you didn't. You did a good job. Let's get this started now!"

He approached Cooper's house again, and

knocked several times on the front door, but there was still no response. Before forcing the door to Cooper's house open, Amery decided to knock on the neighbour's door, having heard a dog bark.

"You wait here, and Merriweather and I will try next door."

PC Johnson stood outside Cooper's house and waited for them to return. The door was opened by an elderly gentleman with a black and white collie dog.

"Good afternoon!" said Amery, showing his warrant card and clutching the warrant in his other hand "I wonder if you can help us? We are looking for your neighbour, Mr. Cooper. Do you know him?" he asked.

The gentleman answered, "Yes, Mr. Cooper lives next door, but he's in hospital at the moment and I am looking after his dog." He stroked the head of the dog.

"Do you know what hospital he's in?" Amery asked.

"No. I'm sorry. He didn't say, and I didn't ask. He just asked me to look after Bess for him, as he was having a small operation, and would be away for about four days. That was a couple of days ago." he replied, and continued: "She isn't any trouble, although she does need a lot of exercise. I have a fair-size garden, and just throw the ball, and Bess brings it back, and that is about all the exercise I'm capable of giving her. I have to say I don't like having to 'poop scoop', but Thomas left me a gadget which means I don't have to keep bending down to pick it up. I just put a disposable bag on the end and scoop."

Amery patiently listened to him then said, "I'm sorry, I didn't ask your name, sir?"

The gentleman replied, "It's Ivan Morris."

"Mr. Morris," said Amery "do you know if Mr. Cooper has a car?"

Ivan replied: "He has a red car, possibly a VW, but I don't know the number, I'm afraid. I hope it isn't important. I see it most days on the drive, as we are semi-detached, but I've never looked at the number."

"He keeps it very clean, and Bess is only allowed in the boot, where there is a blanket and a dog guard, so she couldn't get into any of the seats. He drove himself to the hospital, so I bet he has to pay a lot for parking when he comes out!"

Ivan certainly needed to talk!

"Mr. Morris, do you by any chance have a key to Mr. Cooper's house?"

"I do!" he replied, "Do you need it?"

"Yes, please!" said Amery, and Ivan Morris took a key off the hooks in the hall and passed it to him.

Amery thanked the old gentleman and said he might be back to speak to him a little later. Then he and Merriweather went next door to Cooper's house, where Johnson was waiting outside, and using the key, they entered the house.

However, the first thing Amery did was to put a call into HQ and ask them to call all the local hospitals in the area and find out if a Thomas Cooper had been admitted for a routine and arranged admission within the last few days. He asked that they also call specialist hospitals within a thirty-mile radius. He wanted to give Cooper the benefit of the doubt at this stage, but really didn't think he was in hospital at all.

Amery spoke to Johnson. "Do you know, PC Johnson, I don't know your first name."

This was really a question to Johnson, and he replied, "It's Stuart, sir."

"Right, Stuart, we need to search these premises with caution. We are looking for anything that might connect Cooper to Sofia's death, and anything that will give us more information about him, including any photographs and info on his car. Chances are he's skipped. We have given him nearly four bloody days, so we need to tighten the net. Let's get cracking here, but be careful!"

The three of them climbed to the first floor and started a methodical search. There were four rooms. A bathroom and WC in one room, and three bedrooms, one of which was obviously the master bedroom which Cooper apparently used, so Amery searched this room. Merriweather took the second double bedroom and Johnson searched the smallest bedroom and bathroom. They opened cupboards and drawers, looked in the beds and under the beds, and searched the curtains and wardrobes. They checked the underside of the drawers and mattresses, and looked for anything unusual and out of place, looking for photographs, documents and, particularly, anything to do with Sofia.

In the bedside locker in Cooper's bedroom, Amery found an address book amongst some other bits of blank paper, a crossword book, a couple of pencils, an old tissue, and some scraps of paper with notes jotted down. He bagged and tagged them all.

Perhaps prints on something, or DNA might be on the tissue. He hoped for something! He opened the drawers, one by one, taking out clothing, underwear, tee-shirts, jumpers socks and pants.

Suddenly Amery found a pair of women's knickers amongst which appeared to be men's underpants. With care, he placed them in an evidence bag, and noted where he had found it. Could they be Sofia's?

He could hear Merriweather and Johnson rummaging around in the other rooms and hoped they would find something useful. In the smallest bedroom, Johnson came across a box with some photographs, and in the bathroom, amongst toiletries, there were a couple of used toothbrushes which he thought might have DNA. He noticed there was no razor or shaving cream, so he suspected that Cooper had taken that with him when he left.

Merriweather wasn't having much luck. He was still searching the other double bedroom. There were no

119

clothes in the wardrobe except for two winter jackets. There were, however, some old shoes. They were size ten. That matched with the footprint size of walking boots from the scene of crime, but there were no walking boots. He took one pair and set them aside for comparison later. A box under the bed was also full of photographs, so they were set aside.

The three men appeared on the landing at about the same time, and Merriweather remarked that he hadn't found any suitcases or travel bags. He asked whether Amery or Johnson had, and they both replied that they had not.

"There is a loft hatch, there." he said, pointing at the ceiling.

They all looked upwards, and Merriweather searched for something to open the loft. He found a pole with a hook on the end against the wall in the corner of the landing, and guessed it was to pull the loft hatch down. Taking it in his right hand, he reached up and adjusted it with his left, so it went into the slot, and pulled downwards, revealing the open loft and ladder. A rope dropped down, which he pulled, and the ladder followed. Once down and secure, he looked at Amery who said with a smirk,

"You found it, you climb it!"

So Merriweather climbed up the ladder and stepped into the loft. He found a light switch and turned the loft light on. A second later he exclaimed,

"My God, guv, I think you'll want to see this lot!"

Amery climbed up the ladder, gasped silently, then said, "Bloody Hell!" as he stared at the sight before him.

While the floor of the loft was just a wooden floor, there were photographs of young women and girls, hung from the beams in the loft with pieces of tape. There was a table and chair in the middle of the loft with more photographs, scissors, felt tip pens and tape.

Some of the photographs on the table had been cut up. Some photographs were mutilated, so it was difficult to see who it was, while some were just cut around the face. Some had felt tip marks around the neck. Some of the hanging photographs were head-and-shoulder shots, and some were full length. He recognised at least two of the young women as Juliette Palmer and Sofia Archer. The photograph of Sofia was one of those on the table. It was neatly cut out around the face with a felt tip mark around the neck.

"We better get the forensic guys in here, Merry!" said Amery, as he made his way back to the loft ladder to descend back onto the landing. Merriweather followed.

Johnson and Merriweather gathered up the items they had collected from the upstairs rooms and, together with Amery, they went down the stairs and into the through lounge downstairs

Amery made a call to HQ. He asked for forensics to attend PDQ, and for them to put out an APB for Thomas Cooper, who was wanted to help them with their enquiries in connection with the murder of Sofia Archer.

Cooper's description was sketchy, as at that point Amery only had what Johnson was able to tell him, and they had little information about his car, other than what the neighbour had told them. But they would continue searching the house for further information, and he radioed HQ to search records for anything they might have.

Meanwhile, Johnson was going through the photographs, looking firstly for any photographs of Thomas Cooper and his car, but also for photographs of other young women who might be possible targets for Cooper.

Merriweather was looking on bookshelves and cupboards for anything that linked him to Sofia, or other young women, and anything that would better identify Cooper or his car. Then, in a bureau tucked away in the corner of the conservatory, he opened a drawer and searching under a variety of papers he found a logbook for a 1997 red VW Golf hatchback, registration number R599 RCJ. He took it to Amery, who immediately put a call into HQ and gave them the information about the car.

"Hopefully that will get us back on track!" said Amery to Merriweather. "Is Johnson having any luck identifying Cooper in those photographs?" he asked.

"He's still plodding his way through them and hasn't come up with any of Cooper yet. But there are plenty of photographs of young girls!" answered Merriweather.

Just as he was about to reply forensics arrived, so Amery went into the hall and opened the door and let them in. He briefed them on the loft room and explained that the three of them were looking for a photograph of Thomas Cooper. He handed them the evidence bag with the pair of women's knickers that he had found upstairs, and told them they had however found several photographs of young women that was very concerning.

He wanted forensics to find anything that linked Cooper to the death of Sofia Archer, and for that matter any connection whatsoever to any other unsolved murders, or assaults on young women.

Within the hour, forensics had organised shielding for the house, and several other officers were attending to assist in the investigation. Johnson had still not found a photograph of Cooper, but was continuing to look through the images.

Amery had gone next-door to see Ivan Morris again, and without giving him too much information told him he might be holding on to the dog for a little longer than anticipated. He endeavoured to put Morris's mind at rest, adding that the police would be around next door for some days to come.

"If you have any concerns, Mr. Morris, just give me a ring." said Amery. He handed Ivan a business card.

"If I'm not available, someone will contact me, so just leave a message. Good luck with the dog - she's very nice!" he added, stroking the dog before leaving.

Amongst the photographs, Johnson had discovered a very blurry photograph of Cooper standing with a couple of young girls, outside what might have been a public house, but it was difficult to tell. The photograph had been given to forensics to see if it could be enhanced, and whether they could possibly discover where it was taken. An Identikit picture of Cooper might work well with the blurry photograph, so Johnson headed off to the station to work on that before heading home. The rest of the photographs were to be taken to the mobile unit, while a nationwide search had been put out for Cooper.

They had left the Cooper's house around six thirty pm. TV crews had already gathered outside and were filming, and a reporter ran to question Amery and Merriweather. Amery replied, "No comment!" to their questions and carried on walking to the car.

"Always the way!" said Amery to Merriweather. "Once the APB goes out, the reporters descend like vultures."

Amery had kept the address book and intended going over it in the morning. He and Merry were now heading back to the mobile unit having spent most of the day at Cooper's house.

Merriweather pulled up outside the unit and the two of them got out of the car. While Merriweather gathered up the boxes of photographs, Amery went straight in, leaving the door open behind him for Merriweather. Corinna had long gone. Peter was still there, but getting ready to leave.

"Do you need me, guv?" he asked Amery.

"No, Pete, I'll fill you in tomorrow. We've just brought back some things from Cooper's house to drop off then that's it for today. We can go over this all tomorrow. You go home and I'll see you at eight am." replied Amery.

Before Thomas left, he helped Merriweather with the boxes and placed them near Amery's desk, then he left for the night.

"Do you need me for anything else tonight?" enquired Merriweather.

"No. Good job done today, Merry!" he replied wearily. "I have a feeling about this bloody case. It's going to go on and on. I bloody well hope they find Cooper sooner rather than later!"

Merriweather left the unit, walked to his car, got in and drove off.

CHAPTER 10

THEIR MEETING

Amery was now alone in the unit. It was only around seven pm and he wondered if Julia was free for a drink tonight. He thought he really needed one after the day they had, so he justified his reason to call her. She answered.

"Hi Julie, it's me, Simon. How are you?" he asked her.

"I'm fine, and it's nice of you to call. You've been busy?" she enquired.

"Just the usual stuff." he replied.

"I saw some TV cameras on the evening news and wondered if that was anything to do with your case?"

"It was. I don't think I can go into detail about it, but if we meet, I can tell you some of it!" He was trying to coax her into meeting him.

"I'd meet you, Simon, even if you don't tell me!" she laughed.

"Ok, Julia. Do you want to go out and eat? I'm not sure if I've eaten today." he suggested, laughing. "It's been one of those hectic days!" he paused "but more later, eh?"

"That sounds good, Simon, but only if we go Dutch!" was the reply.

"We'll see! So where do you want to meet? You choose, as you know the area better than me."

"That pub we met at before is good for food. Then do you want to come back to my place for a nightcap?" she waited for his response.

"That sounds like a plan, Julia. I'm still at work, so I'll nip home first. Shall we say eight-fifteen?" he asked.

"That's very precise, Simon!" she smiled to herself. "I'll do my best not to be late."

"Oh Julia! Anytime around there's fine." He was flustered. Had he sounded over-precise? Was she joking? "Are you OK with that?" he asked, almost in desperation. What was the matter with him?

"I was joking, Simon. Around eight fifteen will be perfect. Give me time to tidy up at home and put a bottle in the fridge." And with that she put the phone down.

"Good grief" he thought to himself. "What a plonker! She certainly does something for me, that's for

127

sure. I'd better get home and shower."

He left the unit and drove home, smiling to himself all the way. When he arrived, he stripped off and jumped in the shower, had a quick shave, put on aftershave and didn't forget the deodorant before putting a pair of underpants and dressing in a pair of dark brown trousers, light brown shirt and tie. He grabbed his brown jacket from the wardrobe and put on a pair of socks and a pair of brown brogues.

He had a quick look in the mirror and gave his hair a comb, popping the comb into his inside pocket and a handkerchief into his breast pocket. He picked up his wallet and put that into his inside breast pocket, grabbed some change from his night table, stuffed that into his trouser pocket and picked up his car keys on the way out.

Arriving at the pub car park at eight twenty, he walked into the bar and looked around, but she was nowhere to be seen. His heart sank for a moment, but he walked up to the bar, sat on a stool, and ordered a whisky and soda, which arrived in no time at all.

He put his own ice in it from the ice bucket on the bar and as he lifted the glass to his lips, he felt a gust of wind behind him and turned. Julia was opening the door and coming into the pub. He smiled. He was relieved. He was happy. She did something for him which he hadn't felt in a long time.

He stood up as she entered, and offered her the stool next to him, motioned to her to take her jacket, and kissed her on the cheek. She was dressed in a navy mini-jacket, which she slipped off and passed to him, revealing a navy vee-neck wrap-around dress that just showed the hint of her upper legs when she walked. The sleeves were three quarter and lace, and she wore flesh-coloured stockings and navy high heel open-toed shoes.

Her long red hair hung over one shoulder and it took his breath away for a moment. She was wearing a smidgen of make-up, a little blusher, a brownish lipstick, and a rose-gold eye shadow, highlighting her large brown eyes. She had a soft gold chain around her neck and wore a slim gold coloured watch on her wrist. She was beautiful.

"What will you have to drink?" he asked her.

"I'll have a Bacardi and coke, please." Julia replied. He signalled to the bartender, who came across and took his order.

"Bacardi and coke, and could you get us a couple of menus, too?" he asked the bartender, who acknowledged him and proceeded to make the drinks. When the bartender brought the drinks across, he also passed them two menus.

Amery asked her, "Would you like ice?" as he reached for the ice bucket on the bar.

"Yes, please." Julia answered as she pushed the glass forward towards him. He opened the ice bucket, took out the tongs and took two pieces of ice and placed them in her glass. "Is that enough?" he asked.

"Yes, thank you, that's fine!" she replied, as she pulled the glass back towards her, lifted it up to her lips, and sipped it.

"Now, let's have a look at these menus." said Amery, picking one up from the bar. Julia took the other, and after a few minutes they had decided what they wanted.

"I think I'll have the lamb shank, slow-cooked with red wine and rosemary." he said to the barman. "What would you like, Julia?"

"I think I'll have the same." she replied.

The bar tender took their orders and asked them if they would like to take a table. When it was ready, he would get the waiter to bring it over to them. Amery paid the bill and asked Julia, "Would you like some wine?"

"Better not. I have to drive home, and I have a bottle or two chilling in the refrigerator. That is if you still want to join me for a nightcap?" she queried.

"That sounds perfect for me." he answered.

They walked across to a vacant table, carrying the drinks they had from the bar. When they were seated, she asked him,

"Well, so are you going to tell me about your intriguing case?"

"I am sure you know when we met, we were looking into the murder of a young woman. I'm not sure how much to tell you really. It's been a very busy few days, interviewing kids. Oh! Am I allowed to call them that nowadays? Anyway, as you know, we have scoured hours and hours of CCTV, both at your offices and other places.

Interesting things came to light which I'm sure you appreciate I can't disclose, but what I can tell you is we are looking for a chap called Thomas Cooper and that is why the TV crews were there. It isn't, or won't be, a secret as we have an APB out, and he might be our prime suspect at the moment."

"I can't say much more about it, except my head is buzzing, looking through pages and pages of statements, photographs, and reports, so I am really glad you decided to meet me tonight. The company of a beautiful woman is just what I need." He looked into her eyes, and she blushed as he placed his hand on hers. "Now tell me about you." he said.

"Gosh!" she said. "Me? Well, I was born and brought up in Leeds. I left school at eighteen after A levels. I had applied for university and I had been offered a place, but I asked to defer it as I wanted to travel before university, So I worked anywhere I could, from waitressing to office temping. I even worked at a fun fair for a while. I saved my money, as my parents couldn't help me and I have siblings, so money was always scarce, but I bought a return ticket to Australia. It gave me ten stops, which included the return stop in the UK, and I took eighteen months' trotting around the world."

"It was the best thing I ever did! I met so many

different people, and I did some work in places for pocket money. I was nineteen when I set out and twenty-one when I returned." She paused, as the waiter arrived with their food and placed it on the table in front of them. Amery said thank you, and Julia continued with her story, between mouthfuls of food.

"I was lucky that the university kept my place. I went to Anglia Ruskin University in Cambridge to study psychology for three years. Being a student was fun, but I was a bit older than most of the other students, so I felt somewhat out of place at times. I didn't do drugs and I never smoked marijuana or even an ordinary cigarette. But I did enjoy university. I received a BSc (Hons) and I did consider going on to do a master's degree, but decided I needed to get out and work, and earn money. After all I was nearly twenty-five.

The first job I had was in a factory in Leeds, back home. I was working in the personnel department, but it drove me nuts. It was boring, and the people knew little about the world, but I did stay for nearly a year, For the first few months I lived at home with my parents, then I rented an apartment for the rest of the time." She paused to take a mouthful of food and a sip of her drink.

"Then I saw a job, advertised in Oxford, which was for a human resource manager. I applied and got the job, so I moved to Oxford. I stayed there for eight years, and I did enjoy that job. I met David there, and we lived together for most of that time, but there was no long-term commitment, and then he cheated."

"So I left him and Oxford, and moved up here. I

saw the job advertised for the centre manager and applied for it. I've been here for the past four years. I like the job; I like the people I work with, and believe it or not, it's not stressful, but can be exciting at times."

"Like last Tuesday. I met this extraordinarily good-looking man who just walked into my office." She smiled at him "Now it's your turn!" she said, and giggled a little.

He looked into her brown eyes and said, "A question, first. Did you never want children?"

She blushed and looked down at the table and said, "I thought when I was with David that the time was right, but it never happened." She raised her eyes and looked into his.

"But I'm glad now that we didn't have children. After he cheated, it would have been terrible for the children. Would I have just left as I did, or would I have stayed with him for the sake of the children? I don't know. Anyway, I have three sisters and a brother, and they all have children and are happily settled, one way or another, so I can spoil them as much as I like, and then say goodbye when I've had enough. Now come on, it's your turn!"

She waited for him to start talking and then began finishing her food.

"Well, I'm only a little older than you. I'm forty-two years of age, have green eyes, six foot two inches tall, have all my own teeth, and don't work out as much as I should, and that's because I'm usually too busy." He looked at her, and she frowned at him, saying,

"Come on, life history in a nutshell, please!"

He continued "I left school at eighteen like you did, but went straight to Loughborough University and studied criminology. Funny, because I did look at Anglia Ruskin University in Cambridge, but decided on Loughborough. It too was a three-year course for a BA Hons. and after I qualified, I travelled through Europe for a year with a mate from Uni. We went halves on an old car and hoped it lasted for the trip, which it did, and we actually sold it for ten pounds in France, before boarding the ferry home. We took tents and camping gear, we picked up jobs here and there, from bar work to sweeping floors."

He paused, took a mouthful of food and sip of his whisky, then went on; "I spoke a little French and he spoke a little German and we managed for a year travelling through Europe. We started in France and went to Spain, Portugal, then back through Spain and France to Italy. I loved Italy, particularly liked Sorrento and the Amalfi Coast, but also Rome and Milan. We should go sometime."

He threw that in so suddenly that Julia couldn't interject, continuing, "Then Austria, Switzerland, Greece and Romania. We spent a very short time in the Ukraine. Neither of us liked it much, so we moved onto Poland, then Denmark, Norway, Sweden, and Finland. It was driving, ferries, and at one point we left the car and took trains. We hoped the car would still be there when we returned a month later, and it was. I learned to ski, which I love. Do you ski?" he asked her.

She shook her head, adding "It was something I always wanted to do, but never got around to."

"I'll have to teach you sometime." He said and then went on, "Anyway, after a year of travelling I returned home to Nantwich, Cheshire, but like you I found it dull, and needed something more exciting."

"Anyway, I had this degree, so I thought I would apply to join the Police Force, though now it's the Police Service! I obtained an interview and, in short, was fast-tracked and sent to Bramshill Police College. I did all my police training and came out an inspector. I had to learn from the bottom up, which I actually loved."

"I've walked the beats, been on drug squads, flying squads, and I've been in the murder squad now for some time. All in all, I've done twenty years in the job."

He paused, then continued solemnly, "I was married, no children. Didn't get married until I was thirty-six and had four wonderful years with a lovely woman, but my wife died two years ago, and I haven't been out with anyone since, so now you know why I'm so clumsy. A bit out of practice!" he laughed, and she smiled at him.

Though there was more in both their lives to tell, by the time they had told each other their brief life stories, they had almost finished eating. They both finished their meal without speaking. Nothing else needed to be said about each other, their brief histories had told them all they needed to know about each other, at least for the time being. They seemed to have opened their hearts to one another.

Julia had not spoken about her past to anyone before, and Simon hadn't opened up to anyone about his past and certainly had never spoken about his late wife since her funeral. It felt good to confide in someone again.

When they finished their drinks, she gave him her address. She also arranged that he would follow her to her apartment in his car. It was around ten-thirty by the time they left the pub, and he wondered where those two hours had gone. It was just after eleven pm when they pulled up outside her apartment block. They got out of their cars and locked them. He walked with her to the entrance door, which had a security lock. She punched some numbers into the keypad and the door opened. Usually very observant, he took no notice of what she was punching in on this occasion.

He admired her slender body and her stunning hair. They walked up to the second floor and her apartment. She opened the door with her key, and he followed her into an open lounge area, with a settee in the middle and a coffee table between it and the television which was on a stand. Under it was a DVD player. A music centre stood against the wall near a window. The curtains were drawn and near another window stood a table with four chairs. There was a single armchair that did not match, to the side of the room, and a bookcase filled with books against the wall. He took her jacket off her shoulders and she thanked him, taking it from him and dropping it onto the back of the chair.

"You can hang your jacket over there." she said, pointing to the hooks near the front door. "Do you want red wine or white? I have some white chilling in the refrigerator?" she asked him. As he removed his jacket he replied, "White is fine for me, thanks. Can I help you?"

She was walking towards another room, and he followed. Arriving in the kitchen, she opened the refrigerator and took out a bottle of Chardonnay, which she placed on the kitchen counter. She took a bottle opener from the drawer and handed it to him. "You open, and I'll get the glasses."

He took the bottle, opened it, and while he opened the bottle, she took two glasses from the cupboard. She reached up and took an ice bucket from the top of the kitchen unit, showing her slender legs in the process, then opened the freezer and filled the bucket with ice, and placed the bucket with ice on the counter. He hardly took his eyes off her. After filling the two glasses he passed one to her, and they drank from their glasses. He put the bottle into the ice bucket.

He smiled at her and asked, "Shall we drink here, or on that wonderful sofa in your lounge?"

"The lounge." she replied, walking out of the kitchen with her glass in hand. He followed, carrying the ice bucket with the bottle in it in one hand, and his glass in the other. She placed her glass on the coffee table and walked over to the music centre, turned the radio on to

Classic FM and soft music played. She returned to the settee. He was still standing waiting for her to sit.

He put the ice bucket and his glass on the coffee table, and taking her hand in his he pulled her close to him and gently kissed her as they sat down on the settee. They kissed, and she ran her fingers through his hair. then after a moment or two they stopped.

He reached for her glass of wine and passed it to her, then, taking his own from the table, put it to his mouth and drank a little, while not taking his eyes off hers. She also drank some of the wine, then putting her glass back down on the table, she took his glass from his hand and placed it onto the table too. She took his hand and stood up, and he got up, and she said,

"Please don't think me forward, but. . ." and walked towards another door taking him with her. They entered her bedroom. He kissed her passionately, lifted her in his arms and, using his foot, closed the door behind him.

CHAPTER 11

DAY 5

He left her apartment at four am and drove back to his house, which took him around forty-five minutes. Once more he jumped in the shower, and couldn't stop smiling to himself. He felt like the Cheshire Cat, or the cat that stole the cream. He hadn't felt like this in quite a few years. He got out of the shower, rubbed his hair with the towel, and then wrapped it around his waist. He looked at his watch. It said five am. He set an alarm for six-thirty and fell into his bed.

The alarm woke him, and he got up straight away. No snooze button this morning. He went downstairs to the kitchen, filled the kettle and put it on to boil. He took the coffee from the cupboard, put two scoops in the cafetière, and then went upstairs to the bathroom. He had a shave, a quick wash where it mattered, put on deodorant, cleaned his teeth then put on aftershave. Returning to the kitchen, he sat on a stool, waiting for the kettle to boil, and could not stop thinking about the night before.

He didn't feel hungry. When the kettle came to the boil, he was brought back to reality. He filled the cafetière. After a few minutes he pushed the plunger down, poured himself a mug of coffee, then another, and drank it all until it was gone. He went back upstairs to his bedroom and dressed. He couldn't be bothered to make his bed, or even wash up this morning, which was so unusual for him, but he didn't care today. He picked up his car keys and mobile phone and left at seven-thirty, arriving at the unit by eight am.

Pulling up outside the unit he could see Merriweather's car, and knew he would be working his way through the photographs.

He parked up, said good morning to the PC standing nearby, and went inside. As usual there was a cup of coffee waiting on his table.

"Thanks, Merry!" he said. The door opened and in walked Peter.

"Coffee, Pete?" Merriweather asked.

"Thanks." he replied, as he took off his jacket and hung it up. "I've told the lass to come in at nine am. Hope that's OK with you, guv?" he said to Amery.

Merriweather made a cup of coffee according to the list Peter had put up on the wall, and passed it to him.

"That's fine." he replied, then said "Right!" as they got themselves organised. "Let's see where we are today and if anything has happened overnight. Peter checked the intranet and printed off a sheet for Amery. Passing it to him he said, "Not sure if you will be happy, guv?"

Amery read it and bit his bottom lip. Turning to Merry he said, "Read this." and passed it to him.

It told them that the car Cooper drove had been found at the station car park. It looked like it had been there for at least three days, by the date on the ticket.

"Let's assume he took a train." said Amery. "He would probably have gone towards Peterborough. The other direction is mostly country, and there are no branch lines or interchanges. Peter! Can you arrange with PC Johnson to find out from the station if they know which train he took, and if he got a ticket to anywhere specific?"

"It's a long shot, but by now Johnson might have a better description of him. Arrange for forensics to get his car and give it the once over. Normal procedures."

Peter was still checking the intranet. Looking over at Amery and smiling, he said, "Got a bit of good news, guv! Forensics rushed through that photograph, and Johnson helped with a Photofit, as he was the only one to see him, and it looks like they have a perfect match. I'll print it off."

"Marvellous! We needed a break."

Peter printed it off. Amery studied it and said, "Who would have guessed? Make sure that's been circulated, Pete!"

Peter put in a call to the station and asked Johnson to carry out the task and report back to the unit. Amery took out the address book and started to thumb through it starting with A. Nothing struck him. B. Still nothing. C. "Gloria Cooper, 713 Northampton Rise, Plymouth, PL1 1BA" and a telephone number. "Ah!" he thought "I wonder if she's related?" But he also said it aloud.

"What's that, guv?" Merriweather asked, taking his head out of the photographs.

"Got someone here called Gloria Cooper, but lives in Plymouth. Could be good news, could help, or could be nothing. I'll put in a call to the local station." he replied.

He made a call to the CID in Plymouth, who by now would have received the APB on Cooper and, hopefully, his enhanced photograph. He gave them the information and asked them to visit, and find out if she was related and if so, any history about Thomas Cooper. He put the phone down and waited, While he waited, he thumbed through more pages in the book.

Corinna arrived at nine am on the dot, said, "Good morning" to everyone, while she took off her jacket and put it on the back of her chair. She looked at her 'in' tray, took out some documents, and set about typing them up.

Peter had changed the information on the white-board, and it now concentrated on Thomas Cooper. He put up a copy of Cooper's photograph. All the information about the young men had been put to one side. Merry separated all the photographs of young women from the pictures of scenery, landscapes, buildings, and places that might be recognisable. There were a few photographs of very young children that he put on another pile. This Amery found most frustrating, as there was little they could do while waiting for information to come in.

Around ten am. there was a knock on the unit door. Corinna opened it and was handed a large envelope, which she in turn handed to Peter, who opened it. It was some information from forensics He passed it to Amery.

"Fingerprints found at Cooper's house have been linked to a rape of a young woman in Plymouth, six years ago!" said Amery, out loud.

"Look here, guv." said Merriweather, "I've just seen some pictures of Plymouth Hoe. Amongst them was one of a young woman, who looked about fourteen or fifteen years old, posing in front of the Armada Memorial."

He searched the pictures for the photograph he referred to and when he found it, he showed it to Amery.

"I wonder if this is the young woman involved in the indecent assault." Amery said, as he looked at the photograph.

Then he turned to Thomas and said, "Peter! Contact Plymouth and ask them to fax over a photograph of the victim of that rape. Let's see if it's the same one, or if there are more young women involved."

Peter made the call to Plymouth and within a few moments, the photograph of the young woman was faxed over to them. Peter gave it to Amery, who compared it with the photograph of the young woman in front of the Armada Memorial, but it wasn't the same one as this one and looked a little older.

He passed it to Merry, who took one look and said, "I've seen her in this pile!"

He shuffled them around until he found one that resembled her. This was a photograph of a young women in a somewhat provocative pose, standing on a wooden veranda.

"Here it is, guv! I'm sure that's the same girl!" he said, as he passed it to Amery. "Looks like a pub garden, with decking or something." he guessed.

"Get that photograph faxed over to Plymouth, and ask them where that was taken." Amery said, passing it to Peter.

"Also, tell them that if that is the girl who was the victim of the rape, they need to show her the photograph of Cooper and find out if he was the perpetrator."

Within minutes of sending the photograph, a reply came back that it *was* the young woman who was the victim, and that the photograph was taken at 'The Waterfront', a pub on the Hoe. Her name was Brenda King, and she was seventeen years old.

"Is this a pattern?" queried Amery. "I have a strong suspicion it is, and think we may need to visit Plymouth!"

Merry replied, "Never been there, guv'nor!" and smiled.

Meanwhile, at about nine-thirty am, PC Johnson entered the unit. Removing his helmet, he waited. Then, opening his pocketbook, he spoke to Amery and read out the notes he had made.

"I went to the railway station and showed the station master his photograph and he remembered him. He said Cooper arrived on Wednesday about twelve noon, carrying a large green and brown suede suitcase that had wheels and a handle. He remembered him because he said he was rude to him. He said he was just going to close the booking office for his lunch, having been at work since the first train at six-thirty am. Just as he put the shutter down, Cooper had banged on the window and shouted, "You saw me! Open up!"

"He said that he opened the hatch for him, and sold him a ticket for the one-thirty to Norwich. I asked him what he was wearing, and he said he only noticed he was wearing an open neck shirt, and light-coloured jacket. He couldn't tell the exact colour of his trousers or shoes, and couldn't help me with anything else."

"Thank you, Stuart." He remembered his name! "Get your notes to Corinna, she'll type them up, and get yourself a coffee before you go; but we may need your help later. We'll give the station a call when we need you." Then, turning to Thomas he said,

"Pete, put in a call to Norfolk Constabulary, and also Suffolk, as they are closely linked. Tell them we believe that Cooper took a train to Norwich on Wednesday the twenty-ninth, and they should keep a 'big eye' out for him. Tell them we believe he was involved in the murder of the young woman here, which they should have seen from the nationwide APB, but also that we believe he is a serial predator. See what turns up."

Merriweather continued to sift through the photographs and make individual piles, from photographs of young women to pictures of children, or photos of places, landscapes, or buildings.

"Really weird!" he said to Amery. "All these photographs, and you're not in any of them!"

When Peter finished the call to Norfolk, and then Suffolk, constabularies, he went across to Merriweather and asked if he could be of assistance, to which Merry replied, "See if you have any idea where these photographs were taken!" He picked up the pile of landscapes and buildings, and passed them to him.

"OK. I'll do my best!" said Peter and taking the pile, he moved to another table and started to sort through them.

Corinna typed up the notes from Johnson's book. When she had finished, she handed it back to him, and he left.

Around eleven am, the telephone rang on Amery's desk. He picked it up and answered, "DI Amery here?" and listened, and then said "Yes." He paused. "Yes." Paused again. "Can you fax that over to me?"

Another pause, as he listened, then he said "OK. Thanks. I'll get back to you!" and put the receiver down.

Once again, within a few minutes, the fax machine rattled. Amery went across to the machine and out came a report that he took and started to read as he walked back to his desk.

"Right!" he started; getting the attention of Peter, Merry and Corinna.

"Plymouth have interviewed Gloria Cooper who is, and I stress "is" and not "was", his wife. She tells them that they have been separated for the last six years, after she found out from her daughter that he had tried to molest the kid, who apparently is now twenty-one. So, she was fifteen at the time, but it might have happened many times before. The daughter is his daughter."

"Mrs. Cooper told him he had to leave, or she would report him to the police, and he left, and she hasn't seen or heard from him since. According to this" - he referred to the report – "she hasn't divorced him because it would cost her money, and she had no intention of remarrying, so didn't think it necessary and more importantly, didn't want to tell anyone about what he had done, because she didn't want her daughter to have to relive the situation, and she felt it might be her fault it happened, and she also felt ashamed."

"The DC who interviewed her said he had of course reassured her that it wasn't the fault of her or her daughter. He showed her the photograph we sent over and she confirmed it was him, although she said he looked older, which would make sense."

"The DC went on to say that one of his colleagues was taking the photograph to the lass that was involved in the indecent assault, which of course was about six years ago."

"I can't believe that he only started this six years ago. If he's in his early fifties now - let's give him fifty - then he was forty-four when this all occurred. I bet he started earlier than that! I don't think someone starts to molest or indecently assault at forty-four. He had to have started earlier!"

"I wonder if he always lived in Plymouth?" he went on.

"Those photos, Merry," he said "let's see if we can figure out where they were taken. I bet there are links, and those are his reminders."

Turning to Corinna he said, "Come on girl, you can see if you recognise any of these places!"

Merriweather reorganised his piles of photos, and moved them so that they could concentrate on the photos of landscapes, buildings etc, that Peter had taken. He spread them back over the table, and Corinna came across, and the four of them studied and moved them around, picking them up and examining them, trying to figure out where any of them had been taken.

Corinna picked one up and said, "Is this Paris or Blackpool?" as she swivelled both the photograph and her head, looking at the picture.

Then she passed it to Peter who, looking closely at it, said, "I think that's Blackpool Tower."

Amery put his hand out. Peter gave him the photograph and, after looking at it, Amery said, "I agree. I think that *is* Blackpool Tower!"

"Now the problem is to work out when it was taken. Are there any photographs of young women that you can make out, who might be in Blackpool?"

"I don't know!" said Merriweather. "I'll have a look through them and see what I can find." He then started to look through the pile of photographs of young women. He was looking for any pictures that might have a background which included the Blackpool Tower, or any part of it, and it didn't take him long to find something that looked exactly like that.

A photograph of a young woman about sixteen or seventeen years of age, dressed in three-quarter tight black leggings and white, very short, semi-flared skirt, and a short-sleeved black blouse with padded shoulders that had the top two buttons open, just revealing a little of her breast.

She was leaning against what appeared to be a red post box, and behind it he could just see metal structures of what might have been the lower parts of Blackpool Tower. It looked like a sunny day, so the assumption was it had been taken during the summer.

He passed it to Amery, who studied it, turned to Peter, and said, "You'd better put a call to Blackpool and find out if there is any connection there. Speak to CID. Tell them we have no idea when the photographs might have been taken, so it might have been a long time ago, but you can get the photo over to them."

Corinna interjected, "Excuse me, sir, but from those clothes I think it might be around the nineteen eighties!"

Amery looked at her and the photograph again, and replied, "Thank you, Corinna, that might be very helpful." Then, turning back to Peter, he continued, "Tell them it might be in the eighties." and after a few minutes, he said, "By the way, Peter, have we heard from WPC Scott? How is she doing and how are the family?"

Peter told him that she had been going to the house every day, and staying with the family to give them support. There was still a PC outside the house to ensure the family's privacy and security.

Amery asked him if the underwear that was found at Cooper's house was still with forensics, and if they had identified to whom it belonged, and could they fax over copies of the photographs of the young women that were in the loft.

Peter replied again, "I'll make the enquiries with Blackpool first, then I'll find out about the underwear and the photos, guv."

"OK." said Amery, "You contact Blackpool, and

Merry can contact forensics about the knickers and the photographs."

Merriweather immediately put in a call to the forensics department at HQ and made enquiries. Forensics told him they had been unable to establish anything yet, though they were working on minute samples of soil or dirt found on the outside of the knickers, and samples of the soil where the body was found, but no results yet. Meantime they would organise copies of the pictures from the loft and get them over to the unit.

It was now past mid-day and Corinna was still looking through the landscapes, buildings and photographs of scenes. She asked, "Does anyone want coffee?" to which Amery replied, "Good idea Corinna, let's all have a cup of coffee!"

"Peter, put a list up over there!" - he pointed towards where the kettle stood - "and while you're about it, go ask the PC outside if he wants one."

Corinna smiled as she thought, "That's a nice thing to do!"

Amery continued, "Anyone fancy pizza? I'm bloody hungry!"

Merriweather and Thomas looked at each other with surprise, then they looked at Corinna and turned to Amery.

Merry spoke first, saying, "Great, guv. I'll have some of that!" Thomas said, "Yes thanks, guv." and

Corinna asked, "Did that include me, sir?"

Amery turned to her and said, "Of course, Corinna, but you've got to organise it. Just let me know how much, and I'll give you the money."

She replied, "Thank you, sir. Any particular type?"

He replied, "Anything you fancy, but enough for all of us!"

Corinna telephoned the only place she knew, which was the restaurant in the mall, and ordered four pizzas of varying types, saying she would come and collect them, but needed them PDQ. She asked how much and told Amery that she needed thirty-two pounds as they were eight quid each and that she would go and collect them. He gave her the money. Without making the coffee, she left the unit, got into her car and drove to the mall.

Amery turned to Peter, saying, "Pete, make the coffee when you've made that call, please." Thomas nodded.

Meanwhile, Merriweather continued searching for any buildings or photographs of landscapes he recognised, and waited for the photographs from the loft to be sent over.

Corinna arrived back at ten past one pm and passed the pizzas around, together with some paper napkins she had picked up. She made an extra coffee for

herself and one for the PC outside, the others already
having received theirs from Peter. They all cleared a space
for the food and stopped working for ten minutes, to eat.

Amery was famished. Last night had now given
him an appetite, and while he was eating a piece of pizza,
he was grinning to himself. Merry noticed the grin and
said to him, "You OK, guv? Something on your mind?"

It brought Amery back to the matters in hand. He
smiled and said to Merry, "Nothing in particular. But this
pizza is pretty good!"

He turned to look at Corinna, who acknowledged
him with a nod and a smile, as she stuffed a piece of pizza
into her mouth and wiped her mouth on a paper napkin.

Around two pm, Plymouth CID called Amery to
tell him that the photograph he had sent over, of the
young woman outside the pub, was the young woman who
was indecently assaulted, and incidentally, the photograph
of the girl in front of the monument was in fact Cooper's
daughter, Marilyn.

At two-fifteen pm, a call came in from Blackpool
CID to say that the young woman in the photograph was a
Sarah Mulligan. She was sixteen years of age at the time of
the photograph, and she was raped in nineteen eighty-two,
and did they have any further information? Peter had
taken the call, as Amery was on the call to Plymouth CID,
so he said he would get back to them.

When Amery got off the phone call with
Plymouth, saying that he may be coming down to further

interview Gloria Cooper, he then telephoned Blackpool back. He faxed them the photograph of Cooper, reminding them that they should have already received one, as there was the APB out on him. Blackpool CID said there appeared to be a similarity to the description that the victim had given, so they would take her the photograph and ask her if she recognized him, and would get back to him.

Amery put in a call to the Chief Constable of Cambridgeshire at HQ asking for permission for him and Merriweather to travel to Plymouth, within the Devon and Cornwall Constabulary. He explained the circumstances, saying he primarily wanted to interview Gloria Cooper in connection with the murder of Sofia Archer, but he would also be able to assist the Plymouth CID with their investigation of the indecent assault from nineteen ninety-two, and that the two cases were related. Also that Plymouth knew he wanted to carry on further investigations with the prime suspect's wife.

Within an hour he received a fax confirming he and Merriweather were able to make the trip, and giving them three days to carry out the enquiries, but should they need longer, to contact HQ and report.

Turning to Merriweather, he said, "Merry, can you be ready to drive to Plymouth tomorrow?"

Merriweather replied he could, and Amery continued,

"We can leave at ten am. We'll probably get to Plymouth around four or five pm. I'll speak to Plymouth

CID, tell them we are coming, and get recommendations for a hotel. We can stay two nights, interview Gloria Cooper on Sunday, and travel back on Monday morning."

Amery put in another call to Plymouth CID and said he would be travelling up the following day and asked for recommendations for hotels. The officer he spoke to said he was DI John Graham, and he could arrange accommodation for the two of them, as he had contacts, and would meet them when they arrived. He gave them his mobile number, to call when they were on the outskirts of Plymouth.

Amery gave him his own mobile number in case he had any info for him, and asked if he could confirm with Gloria Cooper that she would be available on Sunday, the second of August, for interview either at her house or the station, whichever was most convenient for her. He said he also would like to talk to her daughter, Marilyn, and asked for a female CID officer to accompany them. DI Graham said he would make all the arrangements for him, and said he would call Amery to keep him up to date.

Corinna made some more coffee for them around three-thirty, which they drank as they continued to go through the photographs, endeavouring to recognise where they might have been taken.

Thomas had made up the white board with the photograph of Sarah Mulligan and written, "Rape - Blackpool 1982". Next to it and '1992' he had put the photograph of Brenda King and written "Indecent Assault - Plymouth 1992", and in brackets next to it he had written "(and Marilyn Cooper!)".

At five pm. Amery said, "Peter, tomorrow I want you to continue through these photographs, and see if you can match any of them, and anything else you can find. Have a word with Johnson and see if he is on duty. Arrange for him to come and help. Tell his boss we need him next time he's on, because he might be able to identify any of the young women from the photographs that were in the loft, and he can help to identify the places in the photographs. Tell him we need the bodies!"

Then he turned to Corinna and said, "Do you want some overtime, lass?" She nodded.

"OK, come in tomorrow and help Peter. He'll tell you what to do, and you can make him coffee!" he said, laughing, then added, "Or perhaps he'll make it for you!"

"Ok, everyone, let's call it a day, and if you find anything tomorrow, let me know straight away, and if I need anything, I'll call!" Turning to Merriweather he said, "Merry, pick me up from my place at ten am, and we'll go straight from there."

With that, he picked up his briefcase and, opening it, put the address book inside, together with a notepad and a couple of spare pens, and walked out of the unit and got into his car.

He arrived home at five forty-five pm. Dropping his keys on the worktop in the kitchen, he placed his briefcase on a chair, then picked up the phone and called Julia on her mobile. She answered after a few rings.

"Hi Simon. How are you?" she asked.

"I'm fine, honey." he replied, "I was wondering if you wanted to meet up tonight? I have to go to Plymouth tomorrow for a few days so might not see you till next week."

He felt he was rambling again, but hoped she had understood what he had said.

She replied, "I'm still at work but should finish in about fifteen minutes. How about you meet me at my place and I cook us a meal tonight with a couple of glasses of wine?" Then she added, "Like last night." And he could almost feel her smiling!

"That sounds good. But I'll pick up the wine, OK?" he replied.

"OK, fine, but come over about seven-thirty to give me time to pick something up and get cooking." And with that she ended the call.

Amery undressed, throwing his dirty clothes into the linen basket, had a shower, shaved, and cleaned his teeth. He splashed on a decent amount of aftershave and deodorant, changed into clean clothes, and quickly made his bed, as he hadn't done it in the morning. He went downstairs to the kitchen and filled the kettle, and put it on to boil. Returning upstairs to the bedroom, he opened his wardrobe and took out a small suitcase from the shelf on top. Placing it on his bed, he opened his drawers and took out three pairs of underpants, three pairs of socks, three shirts, two pairs of trousers, two ties and one pair of brown shoes. He went to the bathroom and took a toiletry bag from the bathroom cabinet and filled it with shower gel, shampoo, deodorant stick, aftershave, toothbrush and toothpaste, shaving cream, razor and bathroom sponge.

"That should do." he thought to himself. "If I need anything else, I'll pick it up in the morning."

Then returning to the bedroom, he put the toiletry bag in his suitcase, looked for his spare phone charger and seeing it, unplugged it, and put it in the suitcase. He left the suitcase on his bed, but didn't close it just in case he wanted to add anything in the morning. He had no intention of returning to it until then.

Returning to the kitchen, the kettle had boiled, but he remembered, and discovered his mug and the cafetière that he hadn't emptied, and washed up from the morning. It only took him a couple of minutes to get it ready and add the coffee and boiled water. He left the used mug in the sink and took a clean mug from the cupboard. Pushing the plunger down slowly, he watched the ground coffee whirling around in the dark water until it finished at the bottom of the glass container. He poured himself a mug of it and sat on the stool, waiting for it to cool a little before he drank it.

Once he finished the coffee, he returned upstairs to the bedroom, and took a pale blue shirt from the drawer and hung it on hanger with a pair of dark blue trousers. He took a blue tie and slipped that over his trousers. He opened his sock drawer and took out a pair of black socks, placed them inside a pair of black brogues, and finally slipped a dark blue blazer-type jacket on top. Putting the hanger back into his wardrobe and leaving the shoes on the shelf below, he closed the wardrobe.

Checking his watch, it showed seven pm. He glanced around his bedroom, put his jacket back on, picked up his wallet and keys, and left his apartment. Once again, he had left the half-filled cafetière on the worktop with another empty coffee mug.

He stopped at an off-licence on his way over to her apartment and, looking at the wine in the shop, he decided on a bottle of Bollinger. He didn't know what she was cooking, so champagne would go with anything. Then he remembered she had Chardonnay the night before, so he picked up a chilled bottle of that from the refrigeration unit as well, just before he paid at the till.

Arriving at her apartment block at seven forty-five, he rang the security bell next to the keypad and she answered, "You're late!" in a satirical but funny voice, and buzzed the door open.

He went in and climbed the stairs to her apartment on the second floor. Her door was open, and he walked in and closed it behind him. Taking off his jacket, he hung it on a hook beside the door, saying, "I'm sorry I'm late! It took longer than I thought, what with stopping off at the off-licence," He walked towards the kitchen, noticing the ice bucket with a bottle of chilling wine sitting on the table, "but I hope this makes up for it!" and handed her the two bottles.

She was stirring a pot on the stove, but looking at him. She left the pot to take the bottles from him, and put them both in the refrigerator,

"Oh, thank you!" looking at the bottle of Bollinger "That's very generous, and will be absolutely delicious with dinner."

She closed the refrigerator door and turned to go back to the stove, but he put his hand on her arm, gently pulling her close, and said,

"Good evening!" and kissed her gently on the lips.

She responded by slipping her tongue into his mouth and moving it back and forth against his, and he kissed her longer and more passionately, holding his arms around her, and running his one hand up against her neck, and his other just below her waist, pulling her closer.

At first she played with his hair in her fingers but then she began gently pulling away, saying, "I need to finish this cooking. Why don't you pour us a drink? I've already put a bottle in the ice bucket. Or would you prefer a whisky and soda?

"No. Wine is OK and we can have the bubbles with dinner."

He walked out of the kitchen towards the music centre, calling out, "Shall I put some music on?"

"That's a good idea. And would you bring me a glass of wine please? Then take your shoes off and relax." she answered.

Dutifully, he did as she had asked, but not before tuning the radio on the music centre to Classic FM. He poured two glasses of wine, and in stockinged feet took one into the kitchen, placing it on a worktop for her without saying a word. Returning to the other room, he sat on the settee, took a sip of his wine, placed the glass on the coffee table, closed his eyes, and listened to the soft music.

He must have dozed off for fifteen minutes or so, for she had to gently wake him. When he opened his eyes, he smiled to see the radiant beauty standing in front of him. She said,

"Dinner is served!" and she smiled back.

"I'm sorry," he said as he stood up, "I must have dozed off."

He turned to the table and saw a meal laid out. He thought it looked delicious, lamb chops with dauphinoise potatoes and purple stem broccoli, and she had already stood the Bollinger in the ice bucket, and poured out two champagne flutes-full. He held her chair out for her and after she sat, he took a seat himself and picking up the champagne flute looked across at her and said,

"To a wonderful meal and a wonderful evening!"

The champagne flutes chimed as they toasted each other. It was a grand meal - he couldn't remember when he last had dinner cooked for him - and it was a wonderful evening.

CHAPTER 12

PLYMOUTH

He left her apartment at seven am. the next morning and drove home, showered, changed into the clothes he had got ready on the hanger the night before, and closed his suitcase. He put it by the door in the hall with his briefcase, rinsed out the mugs and cafetière from the night before, and made himself a jug of coffee.

He sat down in the lounge and turned the TV onto the news channel. He drank his coffee while waiting for Merriweather to pick him up. Just before Merriweather arrived, he went upstairs, tidied his bathroom, and made sure his bedroom was tidy. Then he went back downstairs, washed up his coffee mugs and the cafetière.

"You never know when I might have someone over!" he thought to himself, thinking about Julia.

He dried them and put them away in the cupboard, returning to the TV before Merriweather arrived at nine fifty-five am. Turning the TV off, he picked up his bag and briefcase, leaving his car keys on the worktop in the kitchen, and met Merriweather at the car.

"Nice morning for a drive, guv!" Merriweather said to him as he opened the passenger door.

"Very nice, Merry!" he responded "Let's take a leisurely drive to Plymouth and stop for lunch somewhere along the way."

"Great, guv, I can do that. I filled the car up, so we are ready to go." Merriweather said, as he took Amery's bag and briefcase and put it into the boot of the car, before he got in the driver's side, started the engine, and they set off for Plymouth.

"I reckon we can make Bristol by about one o'clock, and stop there for lunch. Is that OK with you, guv?" asked Merriweather.

"Yup, Merry. You're the driver, so you are in charge this morning. If I fall asleep, wake me at Bristol!"

Amery buckled up his seatbelt, tipped his chair back and closed his eyes. It was just over three hours later when Merriweather woke him.

"We have arrived, guv. Hope this pub is OK!" he said, as he pulled into the car park of the Swan and Anchor.

"Good God, Merry! Have I been asleep that long?" said Amery, surprised.

"You have, guv. I think it must have been a busy night!" replied Merriweather, as he switched the engine off and got out of the car.

Amery followed him, stretching as he stood up, in to the car park. Merriweather locked the car, and the two of them walked into the pub. They had a beer, ordered food, and stayed in the pub for almost two hours before they set off again.

Amery was now well rested and wide awake for the rest of the journey. He and Merriweather talked about the case until they eventually reached the outskirts of Plymouth, around four forty-five.

Amery telephoned DI Graham, who gave him directions to the Crown Plaza Hotel. He told Amery that there was parking at the hotel, and although the rooms were normally eighty quid each, he'd got a deal, and had negotiated both rooms for two nights for a hundred and sixty pounds, including breakfast. He said he would meet them in the bar at the hotel at six pm.

They arrived at the hotel at five minutes past five and parked in the car park. Collecting their luggage from the boot of the car, they entered the hotel through its back entrance. At the reception desk Amery gave his name, saying that the bookings had been made by DI Graham from the Plymouth police department. The staff were fully aware of the arrangement and gave them adjoining double rooms on the fifth floor, with views over the Hoe.

Amery took his briefcase. The porter carried their travel cases to their rooms and handed them the keys, with information about the times of breakfast. He told them the bar was on the ground floor and very near the reception area. Amery thanked him and put a five pound note in his hand as he closed the door to his room.

First knocking on, and then opening, the inter-communicating door, he spoke with Merriweather. "I think DI Graham did us a favour here. I owe him a drink! I'm going to have a quick shower, and I'll meet you in the bar at six." And as Merriweather acknowledged him, Amery closed the door.

He showered, changed his underwear, putting his shirt and trousers back on. He straightened his tie, put on his socks and shoes and went down to the bar at five fifty-five. Merriweather was already there, drinking a pint of beer, and had a whisky and soda on the bar, waiting for him.

"Thanks, Merry! I'll get the next one." said Amery, as a tall young man approached them, smiling, and said,

"You must be DI Amery and DS Merriweather. Pleased to meet you, I'm John Graham." offering his hand to them. Amery took it and shook hands with him, introducing himself, and saying,

"Simon Amery, and Keith Merriweather or Merry! Very pleased to meet you. What can I get you?"

Amery ordered him a whisky and soda, and another for himself, and a beer for Merry. They took their drinks to a relatively secluded table in a corner of the bar, where they could talk about the interview the following day. Graham had arranged to pick them up at ten am. He would bring a very experienced female detective with him, and they understood the situation.

Amery said, "We need to get more information from Cooper's wife and daughter. We believe he was involved with the murder of a young woman on our patch, and it looks like he is involved with at least two rapes or indecent assaults. My gut tells me there will be more!"

"You know we have put out an APB, and a description, and a photograph of him, and my squad are working through a huge number of photographs from his home. There are places we are trying to identify and loads of pictures of young women. That's how we found the one from down here."

"What I don't understand is, why hasn't he changed his name? It seemed too easy to have so suddenly found his wife. Perhaps he thought he wasn't going to get caught, but there's more to this, I'm sure!" He looked across the table to John Graham.

"I think you're right. We would never have connected him until you sent those pictures across. We spoke to Brenda King, who is twenty-three now. She was only seventeen at the time and she said it brought back so many bad memories when we showed her his photograph, but she's glad we have identified him and said she would identify him personally if, sorry, when we get him."

"For a long time she blamed herself, but because she reported it, she was able to seek counselling and has gone on to make a good life for herself. I understand there was a connection with Blackpool too?"

"Yes." Amery replied. "A rape in Blackpool, seventeen years ago, with an sixteen-year-old. She is now about thirty-two. The CID there confirmed he was the perpetrator, after showing the woman his photograph."

"I am hoping that they showed her several photographs, and she picked him out. Could be dodgy if they only showed her his photo. I so want to get this bastard, and as I said, there must be more victims. So, if the victims have reported the rapes or indecent assaults, I am optimistic his photograph will help in identifying him. I just hope there aren't any further murders. These girls were so young!"

They stayed at the bar for a couple of hours, and then Graham took them to a local Chinese restaurant for dinner. Amery insisted on paying saying, "It's on expenses, but I must get a receipt."

After that they returned to their hotel and had a nightcap at the bar.

Before going to their rooms, Merriweather said to Amery, "You know, guv, the more I read into this, the more I think he did more than just try it on with his daughter. I think she may come clean, now she is so much older."

Amery replied, "I was thinking the same thing myself."

They finished their drinks and went to their rooms at around ten thirty pm. Amery suggested to Merriweather that they meet at eight am and go to breakfast together.

After Amery closed the door to his room, he stood for a moment at the window, watching the lights twinkling in the distance. Though it was dark outside, he could make out where the Hoe was, and the water. It looked quite pretty at night, and of course there wasn't a sound. He realised he hadn't put the light on in the room either, so he crossed to the bed and switched on the light above it.

He took his mobile phone from his pocket and dialled her number. She answered after a few short rings. In a sleepy voice she said, "Hello?"

Amery said, "I just wanted to hear your voice. I hope I didn't wake you." She replied, "You did wake me, but I'm pleased you called. I miss you."

Amery hesitated for a moment, because he missed her too, but said, "I'm sorry I woke you."

"No. It's OK. It's nice to hear your voice too! When are you coming back?"

"Not till Monday. I hope it's Monday. Anyway, that's the plan, but if there is any change I'll let you know." He paused for a moment, then said "Not sure what time, but if you want to meet me that would be great!"

"Call me when you are back and I'll cook dinner for you."

"I'll look forward to that. I'll try to call you tomorrow night, if you like?" he suggested.

"I will definitely look forward to hearing from

you. Goodnight. Sleep tight, don't let the bed bugs bite!"

"Goodnight!" he said with a smile, and ended the call.

He undressed, fell into bed, and slept well until his alarm went off at six thirty am, when he got up, switched the TV in the room on to the news channel, then went into the bathroom, showered, shaved, and dressed. He made himself an instant coffee from the equipment left on the dressing table. It didn't taste as good as the coffee he had at home, but it hit the spot for a morning wake-up. While he drank it, he looked at the view from his window.

It certainly was interesting, and quite pretty. The boats in the harbour bobbing about in the gentle waves, the grassy hills, the lighthouse, and the monument where the photograph was taken. It was a sunny morning, and he hoped the weather would stay nice.

At seven fifty-five am he knocked on the inter-communicating door and called out, "You awake, Merry?"

The door opened instantly. "Yes, guv, just had a coffee and now I'm ready for breakfast."

He held his room key in his hand and walked into Amery's room, closing the door behind him. Amery switched the TV off, picked up his room key, and the two of them went out through Amery's room and up to the penthouse restaurant, where they had the most amazing views over Plymouth Hoe as they were served breakfast.

After breakfast they picked up a newspaper each,

and sat for a while reading the papers, and looking at the view. Amery said, "This is very relaxing, Merry, but we're here for work, so let's get cracking."

They put their papers down, stood up and went to the lift. When the lift arrived they got in and pushed the button to their floor. Merriweather said, "I'll meet you down at reception, guv."

"OK. I've got a couple of things to do first anyway."

It was nine thirty am, so they had half an hour before DI Graham arrived.

CHAPTER 13

GLORIA AND MARILYN COOPER

Graham arrived just before ten am, parked in the car park, and entered the building through the rear entrance. He was accompanied by a young woman in her late twenties or early thirties.

She had brown shoulder length curly hair and little make-up, but a bright red lipstick. She was very smartly but casually dressed, in black slacks and a green blouse, with black mid-length jacket. She wore low heel black court shoes, and carried a green shoulder bag. Graham introduced her to Amery and Merriweather, shaking hands with them both. She was DC Caroline Martin.

Pointing to the empty seats in the corner of the bar area, Amery said, "Nice to meet you, Caroline!"

As they walked across the reception area to the seating area, he turned to Graham and suggested, "I think, for the purpose of this visit, with all due respect, when we visit the Coopers, and after the introductions, we should use our first names. My feeling is, we want to keep this interview, using the word 'interview' loosely, casual."

He paused for a moment as they sat down, then continued, "We want to get as much history and information as possible from Gloria Cooper, and I really want to find out about their daughter, Marilyn. Merry and I have talked about this at length, as you can imagine. We think Marilyn can give us a lot more information about her relationship with her father, and that is where you come in, Caroline!"

He turned to her, and she acknowledged him with a nod.

He continued, "You know this part of the country, John, so it would be helpful if you noted down any landmarks she may mention, and we can discuss them later."

"I have prepared some questions I need to ask, but if you think of anything else that might be helpful, then please ask them while we are here. Merry is really good at making notes!" He turned to Merriweather, who smiled at him and gave a little tut, with a backward nod of his head.

Graham said, "I have brought along a small tape recorder, in case you need to tape anything, or if you do interview either of them formally. I thought this might be useful, as long as we let them know we are recording the interview or conversation."

Amery replied, "Thank you, John, that could be *so* useful! Initially, I just want us to talk to Gloria about her husband and, as I said, Merry can make notes, but if we want to make it formal, or if Marilyn wants to give a statement, we can use it."

"What time have you told her we'll be there?" he asked.

Graham replied, "Ten thirty, and it's only about fifteen minutes from here, so if you are ready, we can go!" he said, standing up.

Amery checked his watch, which now showed ten fifteen am, and he stood up at the same time as Merriweather and Martin. They followed Graham to the car in the car park.

They pulled up outside 713 Northampton Rise, at exactly ten thirty am. As they got out of the car, the door of the semi-detached house was opened by a young woman about twenty or twenty-one years of age.

She was about five foot six inches tall, slim built, and had short dark brown hair cut into a bob. She wore a pair of blue denim jeans, and had a slightly baggy blue cotton blouse and a pair of white sneakers.

She smiled at them, as they opened the gate to the front garden and walked towards the house. When they were almost at the door, she said, "Hello! My mum and I were expecting you! I'm Marilyn. Please come in."

The four of them followed her into the house. It was a very tidy house, and open plan, so as soon as they entered, they were in the main living area, which had a dining area at the far end, with French windows that led to a garden. The kitchen appeared to be through a separate door off the living area.

As the door opened, a short plump lady in her forties appeared, wearing a pair of furry slippers. She had greying hair, and wore an apron over a flowery dress. As she entered, she said, "I'm Gloria. I'll be pleased to help you, in any way I can. Would you like a cup of tea or coffee?"

Amery answered for them all. "No, thank you, Gloria. I'm Detective Inspector Amery, Simon, and this is Detective Inspector John Graham, DS Keith Merriweather, and DC Caroline Martin. Just call us by our first names."

"Please sit down." she said. "Marilyn, get a dining room chair and bring it over, will you, darling?"

Merriweather, who was nearest, went with her and picked up the chair, brought it forward, and sat on it.

"Make yourself comfortable." he said to Marilyn, pointing to one of the armchairs.

When everyone was seated, DC Martin took care to sit close to Marilyn, and Amery and Graham sat opposite Gloria. Merriweather was to the side, on the dining room chair, and had taken out his pocketbook and pen.

"Gloria," started Amery "I want to ask you some questions about your husband, and hope you can help me. Where did he come from and where did he grow up?"

"I think he came from Lincolnshire, Boston. I'm

sure he told me he lived there, and went to school and college there, but left when he was about twenty-four, and after that he travelled all over the county." She answered without hesitation.

"Does he have any relatives still there, any brothers, sisters, cousins, still living there, or even near you?" Amery asked her.

"None that I know of. He told me he was an only child of only children of only children! We used to laugh at that. That was when we first married, so as far as I knew he didn't have any relatives." She smiled.

"So tell me, Gloria," Amery continued "when and where did you meet him?"

"I met him at a fun fair in Durdham Park, Bristol in nineteen seventy-six. He had been working on some equipment and I had gone there with a friend. He was twenty-eight and I was twenty-one. He was nice and, I thought, quite handsome."

"I was pretty shy in those days, but my friend didn't like him, so she went off on her own, and I stayed with him. He took me home, and we dated for about six months. He went away in between, as he was working, but when he came back, we went to the cinema or for walks in the parks."

"My parents didn't like him, but I don't know why. Anyway, after about six months, he asked me to marry him, and I said yes."

"My parents disowned me, and I never saw them again. Anyway, we moved to Plymouth after we got married, as when he was working here, he found a place for us to live, and the following year I gave birth to Marilyn." and she looked at her daughter.

They could see in her eyes a pride that was tinged with sadness.

She carried on, "I have lived in this house ever since, and he spent lots of time away, travelled all over the country with work. It wasn't until about six years ago that Marilyn told me that he had been very naughty!"

She hesitated and everyone was silent, waiting for her to speak.

"I told him to leave then and there. I said if he ever returned, I would report him to the police, and he packed a bag and left."

"He never returned. I told Mr. Graham that, when he came to see me before!" she said, looking at Graham.

"I understand." said Amery. He waited a moment or two, then asked, "What was his job, Gloria?"

"He was an engineer. He used to work on funfair equipment, so he was always travelling to one place or another."

Amery followed with, "Did he have any hobbies, Gloria?"

"Oh, yes! He loved photography."

She pointed to a photograph on the wall of the Armada Monument on the Hoe. "That was one of his favourites, and the only reason I leave it up is because I happen to like it too!"

"One last question for the time being, Gloria. What was the date of your marriage?" asked Amery.

"We got married on the twenty-second of December, nineteen seventy-six, in Bristol Register Office. I only had one photograph at my wedding, and when Marilyn told me what happened to her, I threw the photograph in a drawer and haven't got it out since."

"There was only him and me and three friends. The one that was with me when I met him at the fun fair, and another girlfriend and her boyfriend, then we went to the pub a few doors away and had a drink, and that was it." She paused. "It seemed romantic at the time. A bit like running away to Gretna Green. That was what I thought at the time."

"Thank you, Gloria. Is there any chance I could look at that photograph?" asked Amery, adding, "That was really, really, helpful! Now I would like to ask Marilyn some questions." he said, turning to face her.

"Perhaps you and John and Keith would like to go into the kitchen and have a cup of tea?" Then turning to Marilyn, he continued, "If you don't mind? And perhaps you could have a look for that photograph."

Gloria stood up and went to a drawer in a tall chest at the back of the room. She opened it, fumbled around, then pulled out a photograph and handed it to Amery, saying, "You can keep it!" She moved towards the kitchen. John Graham and Keith Merriweather followed her.

Marilyn sat upright in her seat, took a deep breath, and said, "I'd like to talk to you!"

Gloria said to her, "OK. If, you're sure." and walked into the kitchen.

They closed the door behind them, and Amery put the photograph in his inside breast pocket without even looking at it.

Amery spoke first.

"Marilyn" he started, "I have a tape recorder and I would very much like to record our conversation, if you don't mind. It will save you having to repeat anything. May I?" he asked her.

"I think that would be a good idea" she replied.

Amery took the tape recorder and passed it to Caroline, who switched it on, saying, "Interview with Marilyn Cooper eleven oh five on the first of August nineteen ninety-eight, at her home, 713, Northampton Rise, Bristol. Present, Detective Inspector Amery" and Caroline said,

"Detective Constable Caroline Martin." Placing the tape recorder on her lap, she nodded to Amery.

"Marilyn, I realise this conversation is going to be difficult for you, but I want you to understand that we are sure that you have done nothing wrong. I know from DI Graham that your mother said that she asked your father to leave when you were fifteen years old, because you told her he had sexually assaulted you! Is that the case?"

She answered, "Yes."

He continued, "You may not have told your mother everything." and he looked at her, and could see the tears welling in her eyes, but continued, "When did he start, Marilyn? You can tell it all to us now, and you just tell us everything." His voice was soft and compassionate, and she answered:

"I think I was about eight years old when he came into my room, one night. He had been in my room many times before. He tucked me in and kissed me good night. I liked him coming to say good night to me and sometimes he read me a story, or tell me where he had been, because he was away a lot, but this time when he came in, he said we had a secret and we had to keep a secret."

"It was only between him and me and mummy mustn't know, because that wouldn't be a secret any more, and I was excited and said I would keep a secret. He said because he was my daddy he was allowed to touch my private parts and he put his hand under the bed clothes and touched my vagina. He was gentle with me, and I could feel him touching me, but he didn't hurt me, and I wasn't sure what he was doing but I remember his smile."

"Then he kissed me like he hadn't kissed me

before. Then he said good night and he left. Nothing else happened for a while, and he went away on another trip, and when he came back, he bought me some presents. When he came to tuck me in, he started to touch me again, but this time he put his finger inside me a little. It didn't hurt at first, but when it started to hurt, I cried a little and he put his hand over my mouth and stopped touching me and whispered to me, "Don't cry, darling, it won't hurt for long."

"Then he touched me again, but didn't put his finger in me, and then he kissed me again and said, "I'll see you tomorrow, sweetheart!" and he left my bedroom."

"I remember burying my head in my pillow and crying. I didn't want to wake my mother and I had promised my father I would keep our secret and I was really confused, but I thought my daddy loved me. He came to my room every night and touched me and kissed me, and sometimes he put his finger in me, but it didn't hurt anymore. I thought he loved me, and then he went away again."

"He did this every time he came home, over and over and he kissed me, and he touched my chest and sometimes he kissed my chest. I was only eight or nine and I didn't have breasts, but he continued to do this every time he came home."

"Then on my tenth birthday…" She paused and looked at Amery, then at Caroline, and said, "My friends came over for tea and after they had all gone, except for one of them, my mother telephoned her mother and whatever was said, I don't know, but she took her home and said she would be back in about an hour."

"Daddy said he had a special birthday present for me, and he carried me up to my bedroom and undressed me and lay me on my bed. Then he took his trousers off and I saw his penis."

She took a deep breath and sighed, "I was ten years old. I had never seen a penis before and his seemed enormous. He opened my legs wide, and he got on top of me and pushed his penis into me."

"I remember it hurt me and I screamed and screamed and cried and cried and tried to resist him, but I couldn't, and he put his hand on my face and said, "Don't cry, sweetheart, it's because I love you." and "You make me do this to you.' and he kissed me."

"He started panting like an animal, and was bouncing on me, and I remember how much it hurt me, and then he stopped and laid his head on my pillow and said, "This is your fault. You make me do this. It's because I love you. But it's our secret, so go to sleep now." then he went to the bathroom and got a towel and wiped me because I was bleeding, and there was wet all around my vagina, then he took the towel away and tucked me in, and I fell asleep."

Tears fell down her cheeks and her nose was running. Caroline passed her a paper tissue, and she blew her nose and wiped her eyes, then went on, "I'm really sorry. I haven't told anyone about this. I always felt it was my fault. He made me feel that way."

"I only told my mother when I was fifteen, but I didn't tell her everything. I only told her he had touched my breast and tried to put his hand on my vagina, but that I pushed him away, and she threw him out. I never told her about what went on from my tenth birthday."

"My mother liked to play bingo sometimes, but could only go when he was home, because she didn't leave me on my own. I dreaded her going and sometimes asked if I could go with her, but my father always found a way for her to go and for him to be with me on our own."

"He would say he wanted to tell me a new story, or tell me where he had been on his adventures, and my mother would smile, as she always thought it was nice he wanted to spend time with me, but as soon as she was gone he would make me go upstairs and get undressed and tell me it was my fault he was doing this."

"He would make me put his penis in my mouth and if I tried to bite him he would hit me on my bare bottom and make me stop, and tell me I was a naughty girl for making him do this. He would put on a condom, and sometimes make me put it on for him and then he would have intercourse with me."

"If I had tried to bite him he would make it hurt me, and do it really hard, and I would often cry, though after a while it didn't hurt anymore, but I didn't like it and he would keep telling me he loved me, but it was my fault this was all happening, and it was our secret, and if I told my mother or anyone else, they would take me away and put me with a family I didn't know, and I wouldn't have any toys or friends."

"I was so relieved when he went away for his work, but every time he came home it was the same thing, and I dreaded it. As I got older, I was able to spend time with a school friend overnight, but I didn't have many friends, so I still had to spend some time with him. I didn't think I could tell anyone, and my school work suffered, and my mother worried about me because she couldn't understand why I wasn't doing well at school."

"Anyway, I eventually told her about him, but as I said she doesn't know the full story. She kicked him out, saying she would tell the police if he ever came back, and we never saw him again, and I was so relieved."

"I was fifteen then, and soon after I started work, I started to read about abusive parents and incestuous relationships. I believed it was all my fault, but I went to a women's support group and they found me a counsellor to talk to and I am now a survivor."

"It is difficult for me to make relationships with men, but I know I will be able to find a healthy relationship sometime, and I no longer believe it was my fault and, although he is my father, if I ever see him again, I think I will kill him!"

She took a deep breath and blew out loudly and Amery said, "Let us deal with him, Marilyn, and don't lower yourself to his level. You are stronger than that, I can tell."

He looked at her and Caroline placed a hand on her arm. "Let the law do the work for you. We will catch up with him, I promise you. You are a very brave young woman!"

He sat forward in his chair, moving closer to her, and suggested, "Do you think it is time to tell your mother everything?"

She replied, "I'm not sure if I can yet." She looked at him, but was no longer crying.

"Well," started Amery "when we find him, don't you want to see him prosecuted?"

She nodded.

"Well, I think you should tell your mother everything. It might come out in court, and she would want to be able to support you. You know, your mum might think it is her fault, and I'm sure you wouldn't want that. Perhaps you could go to a support group for mothers and daughters?"

Amery was clutching at straws, but felt sure that there must be such groups, anyway he knew Caroline and her colleagues would be able to support them both, and he looked over to Caroline, looking for her reaction, and she understood and said, "We can help you, Marilyn! We will be here for you all the way, and if you want me to be with you when you tell your mother, I will be happy to support you!"

"Thank you so much! You know it's the first time I have ever told anyone everything. My counsellor doesn't even know all the details, but I actually feel stronger now, even though I'm crying!" she said as a tear ran down her cheek. She gave a tiny laugh and clutched Caroline's hand.

Amery said, "Is there anything else you would like to tell me or ask me?"

Marilyn answered, "No, I don't think so."

"OK." said Amery "Let's leave it here but if you need anything, or want to talk to anyone, then you call Caroline. She will give you her number and she will keep in touch with me. Let's end this now."

Caroline said "Interview ended eleven fifty-seven."

She pushed 'stop' on the recorder and passed it to Amery, who put it into his pocket, stood up and shook Marilyn's hand.

"You are a very brave young woman!"

Then he went to the kitchen, opened the door and called out, "OK, gentlemen, I think we have annoyed these good people long enough. Thank you, Gloria, I think your daughter might want to talk to you."

Caroline handed Marilyn her card, emphasising that she would take her call anytime, and with that the four of them left the house and returned to the car outside.

Amery spoke first and said, "Anywhere we can go for a pint?"

Graham answered, "I'm driving, so let's go!"
Then he drove them to the Cornubia in Temple Street.

It only took him about ten minutes to get there, and when parked up, the four of them walked in and found a table. Graham went to the bar with Merriweather, and Amery and Martin sat at the table. Amery looked across at Caroline and said, "You did well, girl! Have you dealt with anything like this before?"

She replied, "No! It was quite a shock! I hope I didn't show it. Of course, I've read about this sort of case. In CID here, it's just the usual burglary, theft, arson, stabbings, drugs, and some of them we pass on to other squads, but I felt so sorry for her. She was a very strong young woman and I'm glad she got counselling. If I can help her I will, DI Amery!"

"Thanks. She could do with someone like you to help her." he said, as the drinks arrived.

Merriweather handed them some menus and Graham handed them the drinks. Whisky and soda for Amery, and the same for Graham, vodka and coke for Caroline, and a beer for Merriweather.They ordered food at the bar, and were told it would be brought to their table when ready. Amery paid, and once again got a receipt, saying

"On expenses. Least we can do!"

Having sat down again to discuss these revelations, Amery started, "Unfortunately, it doesn't help us much with regard to Cooper's whereabouts, but it might give us a starting point. If he was an engineer and travelled across the country, he must have left a trail.

186

"Any chance we can go to your office after lunch, and put in a couple of calls?" he asked Graham, who replied, "Of course! It will also give us a chance to look through some of our old files!"

After lunch they went back to Graham's office in Plymouth Police Station. They looked again at the photographs Amery had sent across, and Amery telephoned DC Thomas to see if there was any progress with the photographs, or anything new from forensics.

Thomas said Johnson had recognised some of the young women in the photographs as local girls, and they had found at least one photograph of a place that they felt they recognised. It was of the Herbert Ingram Statue in Boston, Lincolnshire.

They were now trying to link that with any photographs of young women, and still looking at other landmarks or monuments.

Meanwhile, nothing had been heard from forensics, but Thomas reminded Amery that it was Sunday. Amery thanked him, and said to contact him on his mobile if anything else came up.

Turning to Graham, he said, "John. I'm sure you have looked at this before, but if Cooper lived here since nineteen seventy-seven, and the only offence we can see at the moment was in nineteen ninety-two with Brenda King, and a continuous period of paedophilia with his daughter, and we can't be sure when he started, at least not before she remembered when she was about eight years old; do you think there may be more unsolved cases here in

Plymouth?"

"I was thinking the very same thing! Only until today, we didn't know he lived here since seventy-seven, so I'm going to get a search of all our unsolved records and see what it pulls up, with regard to young women, and now even look at children. What a bastard, eh?"

With that John put in a call to records and asked them to start the search.

Amery suddenly remembered the photograph Gloria Cooper had given him, which he had put into his inside pocket, and took it out. It showed Gloria Cooper, the bride, dressed in a floral pink dress and carrying a small pink posy as a bouquet. She was not unlike when he met her in the morning, only very much younger. She was plump but pretty, and had her hair tied neatly in a bun on top of her head. Cooper stood next to her in a grey suit.

He certainly looked a lot younger, but you could see it was the same person. However, no greying hair, and he had what some might say was a 'nice smile'. Amery thought that he hadn't been a bad-looking chap in his youth! The photo was taken in nineteen seventy-six, so he was probably only about twenty-eight years old.

Passing it to Graham to look at, he said, "Can we get this faxed over to my squad?"

Graham took the photograph and examined it. He then went through into another room, returning about ten minutes later, and handed it back to Amery, waving, "It's done!"

"Thank you!" replied Amery. "I'll give them a call."

He took his phone and called the unit. Peter answered and Amery said, "Pete, you'll receive a photograph of Cooper taken in about nineteen seventy-six. I want you to see if we can just use him, and cut the other people out, and circulate that with the APB. Explain it was nineteen seventy-six, but it might help in identifying him in any other unsolved cases. We might be looking to including children!"

"You said you found a photograph from Boston. Herbert Ingram Statue I think you said earlier, well Cooper apparently came from around there, or so Mrs Cooper told us, so make sure that CID in Boston see that photograph of him as a younger man. See what you can do with the photo. Thanks, Pete! Don't work too late, and how's the lass doing?"

"She's really helpful, guv, and Johnson has been a help too, but I'm letting them go soon, as it's been a long day. I've arranged for Johnson to be back here tomorrow, and they will come in at nine am. I'll get on to that photo, guv, I think it just came through on the fax." he replied,

"Pete! If you need me, you have my number." With that he ended the call.

Passing the photograph to Merriweather to look at, he said, "I'm sure you heard all of that, Merry." and turning to Graham, he said "John, I think it might be a good idea if you use it yourself."

"I already took a copy of it, Simon!" he smiled

It was now around five pm, and Amery said, "Not much more we can do here now. I think it's about time to go for a pint and something to eat. What do you think, John?"

"Good idea!" and, turning to Caroline he said "Caroline, fancy joining us?"

She nodded, and picking up her jacket from a chair, she laughed, "I'm already ahead of you!" and they all smiled.

The four of them left the office.

They went to an Italian restaurant that Graham had recommended, knowing that it wasn't far from their hotel. They didn't go to a pub that night, but finished the evening with a couple of drinks at the hotel bar. Once again, Amery picked up the tab in the restaurant, but Graham insisted on paying for the drinks at the bar.

"It goes without saying" said Amery "that you will keep me, or my unit up to date with any progress you make. Meantime, we have got to catch Cooper, and I hope the circulation of his photographs helps us. I want to thank you again, and I hope we can reciprocate at some time in the future."

He paused, then continued, "My round, I think" and the four of them continued to drink until gone eleven pm when Amery said, "I'll see you at eight am for breakfast, Merry. I'm all done in now! Good night all!"

and he went upstairs to his room.

When he got there he decided it wasn't a good idea to phone Julia, as not only was it past eleven pm, but he was a little bit over the eight. He set his alarm for six thirty am with the intention of calling her first thing.

CHAPTER 14

RETURNING

His alarm went off at six thirty am, and he got up straight away and went to the bathroom to pee. He had drunk a lot the night before. But he felt he was making progress with the job, and enjoyed the company of colleagues from Plymouth. He rinsed his hands, then went to the bedroom and put the kettle on. While it boiled, he returned to the bathroom and shaved. Once the kettle had boiled, he made himself a cup of instant coffee and drank it, before showering and dressing. It was now seven am and he took his phone from the dressing table and dialled her number. Julia answered after only a couple of rings.

"Hello Simon. Was it a very late night?" she asked.

"Really sorry, Julia. It was quite a productive day, and pretty full-on, and I'm afraid it turned into a late-night session, sort of saying goodbye to the Plymouth police and thanking them for their co-operation. It was gone eleven pm when I made it back to my room and I didn't want to wake you, again! Am I forgiven?" he pleaded.

"Of course, you are Simon! You hadn't said you would definitely call, so I wasn't worried. I didn't think you had forgotten me so soon!" and she giggled a little.

"How could I do that?" he replied, then continuing, "We will be leaving Plymouth after breakfast, but we want to miss most of the rush hour. I expect we'll stop for lunch somewhere, then we should return about six pm. What do you want to do this evening? Perhaps a take-away?" he asked her.

"Brilliant idea. We still have wine here, so don't bother about getting any more. I'll put the Chardonnay in the refrigerator to chill. Will you bring a take-away in with you, or should we order when you get here?" she asked.

"I'll bring it in with me. I'll go home and shower and change, then pick something up. What d'you fancy?"

"Chinese would be good! I like everything, except anything that might be too spicy. Is that OK with you?"

"Great! I'll call you when I get home and we'll finalize then. Must dash now. Looking forward to seeing you. Take care!" he finished.

"I'm looking forward to hearing from you. Drive carefully!" she replied and put the phone down.

Amery made himself another cup of coffee, before knocking on the intercommunicating door and calling to Merriweather, "Hi Merry, are you decent?"

There was a prompt reply, "Yes, guv, just finishing this coffee, then I'll be with you."

While Amery waited, he gathered up his toiletries from the bathroom and put them into his toilet bag, placing it next to his case which he had put on his bed. He put his clothing in, carefully rolling up his dirty items and stuffing them around the edges of the case. Then he put his toilet bag in and closed the case. He opened his briefcase and took out his notebook, and was reading it when Merriweather opened the intercommunicating door. It was eight am.

"I'm ready, guv!" he said. "I see you've packed already. I'm not quite packed yet, but it will only take me five minutes when we come back from breakfast."

"That's OK, Merry. I was just killing time." he said.

He closed the notebook and placed it back into his briefcase, and then closed that too.

"Let's enjoy this last breakfast before we leave. I'll settle the bill on our way out."

He stood up and walked to the door, opened it and the two of them went upstairs for breakfast and enjoyed the view for the last time. Watching the small boats bobbing about in the water, and the larger ferry off in the distance, and the Monument on the Hoe, brought his thoughts back to the young women involved in this case.

After breakfast they went back to their rooms to collect their luggage. Merriweather quickly packed his bags and the two of them went downstairs. Merriweather took Amery's suitcase and proceeded to the basement car park. Amery paid the bill at the reception desk and thanked the hotel for their hospitality, before joining Merriweather at the car. Amery opened the back door and put his briefcase on the seat, then closing the door opened the front passenger door, and got into the car. Turning to Merriweather he said,

"OK, Merry, let's drive for about three hours, then find somewhere for a break. I don't know about you, but I'm stuffed from breakfast!"

Merriweather responded, "Me too! They had a bloody good selection of food, and the hotel was top-notch. I might even return sometime in the future."

"Me too!" said Amery, as he buckled his seat belt and sat back, thinking about the case.

It was just after ten am when Merriweather pulled out of the car park, headed for the motorway and back to Peterborough.

They hadn't been on the road for more than an hour when Amery's phone rang. He took it out of his pocket and answered it.

"Hello?" he waited for a response then said, pausing in between words, "Right. Right. Right. I thought as much!"

Amery looked at Merriweather and mouthed the words, "It's John Graham!" then, turning his attention back to the call, said, "Thanks, John. Can you send all the info over to my unit?" He paused, then continued, "Thanks. That's great! I'll be in touch with you again tomorrow!" and ended the call.

Amery dialled the unit, and within a few moments Peter Thomas answered, "DI Thomas. How can I help you?"

"Good morning, Peter!" Amery started.

Thomas immediately recognised his voice.

Amery continued, "There should be a fax coming over to you from Plymouth. DI Graham has found a couple of unsolved cases of attempted rape and/or indecent assault from Plymouth and surrounding areas, stretching back to the early seventies. The young women were in their early teens."

"He's going to follow up, if he can, and find the victims who will now be in their thirties, probably, if he can trace them. You got the copy of Cooper's wedding photo, didn't you?" but without waiting for a reply, he continued, "Was it circulated widely?"

"Yes, guv, and we found a photograph of the young woman from Boston in front of that statue of Herbert Ingram we told you about, and we sent that over to Boston with that picture of him from his wedding and we got a hit!"

"They called me back after about two hours and said they had dug up a cold case from nineteen seventy-two. It was the same young woman! Her name was Carole Masters, aged fifteen. They said the photograph of Cooper fitted the description the girl had given at the time. I couldn't believe it, guv, they are trying to trace the young lady involved, but it was a long time ago."

"Good news, Peter! Cooper was an engineer and travelled extensively, working on fun fair equipment and he also came from Boston. So, from the information we have, he would have only been in his early twenties himself at that time. Let me know if what Graham sends you from Plymouth fits anywhere. We won't get back until late, so I'll see you in the morning, but if anything productive comes up, just call me!"

He ended the call. Then, speaking to Merriweather, he said, "We are making some progress, but we need to get a sniff of him soon!"

"Mind if I turn the radio on, guv?" asked Merriweather.

"No, that's OK." he replied.

Merriweather tuned the car radio to a music channel, turned the volume down low, then said, "So, guv, what was the information from DI Graham?"

"He told me they turned up two cases. One from nineteen seventy-eight, and another from nineteen eighty-one, and the 'younger' Cooper fitted the description of the perpetrator."

"Both involved young women around the Dartmoor area. One of the girls was sixteen years old, and the other only fifteen."

"He's sending the details over to Peter."

"Right!" replied Merriweather, and then concentrated on his driving.

It was around one o'clock as they approached Worcester, and Merriweather spotted an Inn along the main road. Before pulling in, he turned to Amery and said, "A pint, guv?"

"Good idea, Merry!" said Amery.

Merriweather pulled into the car park. As Amery got out, he took his briefcase from the back seat and then the two of them walked into the pub. Handing his briefcase to Merriweather, Amery said, "Do you want food, Merry, or just a pint?"

Merriweather replied, "A pint of ale would be good, guv. No food, thanks."

"OK, you grab a table and I'll get the pints." said Amery as he walked towards the bar.

Merriweather found a large table near a window, so he could watch the car, and placed Amery's briefcase on the padded banquette under the window. He sat on a chair facing the window and, as he watched the cars speeding past on the main road, he too was thinking about Cooper and the case.

Amery approached the table, carrying two pints of ale, and placed one in front of Merriweather and the other on the opposite side of the table. Then he sat down on the banquette. Raising the glass of beer, "Cheers!" he said to Merriweather, who responded likewise.

They each took a gulp of the beer. Amery then put his glass down, opened his briefcase and taking out his notebook and pen, started to write. He was making notes which pertained to the conversations he had just had with Graham and Thomas.

He had a pretty good memory, but it always helped to make notes, and the sooner the better. Time sometimes distorted facts and, in this case, there appeared to be numerous names and dates, and Amery knew he wouldn't remember them all.

"I think I'll get a pork pie or sausage roll, guv. Not that I'm that hungry, but I need something to soak up the beer!" and he gave a little snigger.

"Get me something too, Merry. Even if it's some crisps." Amery replied.

"Another pint?" Merriweather asked Amery.

"Just a half for me, Merry." he nodded.

Merriweather went to the bar, returning five minutes later with two jumbo sausage rolls wrapped in paper, and two half pints of beer.

"You know, Merry, I think we'll have time to go straight to the unit, when we get back. I know you're driving, so I'm afraid you will have to drop me back home after, but I promise not to keep you too long."

"No problem, guv! I want to catch up before tomorrow anyway, then I can sleep on the information and take it all in." said Merriweather.

They finished their beer and sausage rolls, then Amery put his notebook and pen back in his briefcase, closed it. They returned to the car, where he replaced the case on the back seat. When they had buckled up their seat belts, they set off again. The traffic was fairly light, so they sailed through to Peterborough with no holdups, and arrived back at the unit at three forty-five pm.

Amery parked the car, took his briefcase from the back seat, and went into the unit. Thomas was surprised to see him, but greeted him and started talking almost immediately.

"Nice to see you guv, though I wasn't expecting to see you until tomorrow. As you can see, Johnson here has been a great help and Corinna too. We've found a few more places that we can identify, and a couple of young women too."

Amery smiled at him. "How about a coffee for two weary travellers?" he said to Thomas.

A voice from behind him said, "I'll make it for you, sir." She got up and went to the kettle.

Amery turned. "Thank you, Corinna. Nice to see everyone!" Then he turned back and walked towards his desk, putting his briefcase on top and opening it, then he sat down.

"Now, Peter, I would like a few more details about the call from Plymouth, and a run-down of where we are, but just let Merry and I get this coffee first. It was a long drive!"

Merriweather, who was following behind, pulled up a chair and sat at the other side of his desk. Amery was studying the board that Thomas was working on, as Corinna brought across two mugs of coffee and said,

"I think I got them right this time, sir!"

Taking a sip of the coffee he replied, "Perfect. Thank you! And how are you, Stuart?" he said to Johnson, who was busy going through the photographs.

"I'm OK, Thank you. Got a few places identified, and recognise a few of the girls in these pictures." he said, pointing to a separate pile of photographs, that Amery recognised as the ones from the loft in Cooper's house.

"OK, Peter, I'm ready now. Let me have what you've got!" Amery said to Thomas. Everyone in the unit turned to Thomas, and listened.

"Right, guv. First, I'll tell you about the info we got from Plymouth, as you know some of it. So, following your investigation, Plymouth identified two unsolved cases."

"The first, in nineteen seventy-eight, involved a young girl called Geraldine Costello, who was sixteen years old. She was hitch-hiking near Tavistock, and was picked up by Cooper. He stopped at Dartmoor and tried to have his way and grope her in his car, but she managed to get out and flag down another vehicle, and he drove off. They didn't have any car number plates, but the girl gave a good description, and it fitted Cooper, and he must have been about thirty years old at that time."

"The second incident was in nineteen eighty-one. Susan Ford, a fifteen year old. Also edge of the moor near Tavistock. He was taking photographs of the moor, and she was walking towards Tavistock, and stopped near him to see what he was photographing. He said he would take her photo and before she knew, he pounced on her and raped her. Then he told her to go home and not to talk to strangers! The girl didn't report the incident for a whole week, but gave a good description of him but, again, no car details. So, Cooper was then about thirty-three."

"Now guv, the photograph we told you about the Herbert Ingram statue in Boston, well we got a picture of a young woman, and as you can see"- he pointed at the board - "we got a positive response from Boston from a young girl, Carol Masters, who was fifteen at the time in nineteen seventy-two. She was sexually assaulted by Cooper, who was probably about twenty-four himself then."

"So in chronological order, we got Carol Master, fifteen, in a nineteen seventy-two sexual assault, then Geraldine Costello, aged sixteen, but she got away, in nineteen seventy-eight. Next, we got Blackpool, and Lancashire Police confirm a sixteen-year-old Sarah

Mulligan was also sexually assaulted in nineteen eighty-one and Cooper's description fits there too. Then it changes, as also in nineteen eighty-one, he rapes Susan Ford, fifteen, but this time it is back near Tavistock."

"We got seventy-two, seventy-eight, eighty-one, that's two in nineteen eighty-one, and from what you say nineteen ninety-two, his daughter and Brenda King and these two were also rape. The others we have identified were indecent or sexual assault. I've put them up chronologically and we still have more photographs, and are waiting responses from those forces."

"Regarding Norfolk and Suffolk. They have circulated his present description and his photograph to all their stations, but so far no results." He stopped and took a deep breath.

"Any coffee for me, Corinna, please?" he said.

"Sorry Pete, I've made it; just forgot to give it to you. Here you are." she said, picking up one of the mugs and passing it to him, then passing another to Johnson and taking one for herself.

"Peter, have you heard from Scott?" Amery asked him.

"She's OK. I spoke with her this morning, and she said the family are naturally still upset and want to plan a funeral for their daughter, but she has explained they have to wait a while longer. She asked if they perhaps wanted to speak with a vicar or a priest, and perhaps have a memorial service for her while our investigations go on, and the family are thinking about that. She says she feels she needs to stay with the family a while longer, but she doesn't stay overnight. She leaves at ten pm and returns at eight am. Meanwhile there is still a PC outside to stop press intruding on the family."

"Thanks for that, Peter. When you speak to Scott again, tell her I appreciate her thoughtfulness with the family." said Amery.

Then he called, "Corinna?" and as she looked over, he said, "I have a tape that needs typing up, but I have to warn you, it isn't pleasant, so if you don't feel up to it I can ask someone else to transcribe it for me." he waited for her to answer.

She looked across at him and could see the pain in his eyes, so she guessed it was a difficult tape. However she replied,

"I'll do it!" and he took the tape and the recorder from his briefcase.

She walked across, took it and returned to her desk.

"It doesn't need completing tonight, so just do what you can, and try to get it finished tomorrow, please." Amery said to her gently. By this time she had put on her earphones and started typing.

Amery studied the board, looked around the unit and watched everyone working busily. He knew they were all hoping that Cooper was captured soon, and that there weren't too many more incidents, but he guessed there would be. After a while he looked at his watch, and it was now five pm. He looked again around the room and said,

"Ok people, it's five pm. Go home, relax, have a few drinks and be back here at eight am tomorrow. You too, Corinna!" he said in a raised voice, and she removed the earphones. "Go home and be back eight am tomorrow." he repeated to her.

Then everyone got themselves organised and left the unit. Merriweather drove Amery to his house, and dropped him off, saying,

"See you in the morning, guv!" before driving off.

After going inside, Amery put his suitcase on the worktop in the kitchen and opened it. He took out his dirty clothing and threw it into the washing machine, then closed the suitcase and took it with him upstairs, leaving his briefcase in the hall. Emptying the suitcase, he carefully put the remaining clothes away, and his toilet bag onto the bed. He put the case back on the shelf in his wardrobe, and then undressed and walked naked into the bathroom, taking the toilet bag with him.

He ran the shower and as the bathroom steamed and the mirror became foggy he stepped into the shower and placed his hands on the wall in front of him. He felt the hot water pounding on his back. He closed his eyes and images of the last few days ran around in his head. He sighed, and stood there for a few moments, before opening his eyes and taking the shampoo and washing his hair, and letting the soap and hot water run down his face and over his chest.

The water fell like heavy rain, gathering in the foot of the shower tray before twirling down the drain. He grabbed the shower gel and washed his body, before he turned the shower off and stepped out and dried himself on the towel that hung on the rail next to him. Drying his hair and body, he wrapped the towel around his waist, cleaned his teeth, had a shave, then splashed cold water on his face before applying aftershave and deodorant.

He went to the bedroom and put on clean and casual clothes. He took the clothes he had removed earlier downstairs and put them into the washing machine. Taking a scoop of soap powder from the cupboard and placing that in the dispenser on the machine, he switched it on.

It was now six thirty pm, and hoping Julia would be home from work by now, he called her. When she answered, he was greatly relieved to hear her voice. It gave him a little boost of happiness, as the last week had been a strain, and very depressing for him. He had never really got used to having to internalize his feelings. Had he only known her for just over a week? He had been able to talk things through with Charlotte. She had been a good listener, even though her job was high-powered and stressful. Since she died, he hadn't been able to do that at all.

He often talked to himself when he was alone. Somehow it helped to say things out loud, even if no one was listening, or particularly if no one could hear. Sometimes he sang, though he knew he didn't have a very good voice. But hearing Julia's voice brought a smile to his face as he asked, "Good evening, Julia! Now what would you like in Chinese?"

She gave him her order and he arranged to pick it up and take it over.

"I'll be about an hour. Keep the wine chilled!" and he ended the call with, "I'm looking forward to seeing you, beautiful lady."

Amery telephoned a local Chinese take-away, put the order in and collected it, on his way to Julia's apartment.

That evening, they ate, drank and made love. There was passion and pleasure.

He returned home at five thirty am the following morning.

CHAPTER 15
DAY 9

It had now been nine days since the murder of Sofia Archer and there had been serious revelations regarding the case, but as yet, no sign of Cooper. Amery drove to the unit and arrived at seven fifty-five am, having been home, changed, showered, and picked up his briefcase. There was one car outside when he arrived. Thomas was already there.

As Amery entered the unit, Thomas immediately said to him, "A bit of good news, guv! Fax came in overnight, there has been a sighting of Cooper in a village called East Dereham in Norfolk. It's about thirty-five miles away from Norwich, and on a bus route. A local bobby saw him yesterday and he reported immediately."

"At last!" exclaimed Amery. "A break!" He walked to his desk and put his briefcase on the table. "Get hold of that bobby, or his boss, on the phone for me, please."

As he was talking to Thomas, he opened his briefcase and took out the address book. Skimming through the pages he found an address for a James Turner at, "21 The Loke, East Dereham Norfolk, NR19 1AG". He continued flipping over the pages in case there were any other addresses in Dereham or Norfolk, but he couldn't find any more.

Thomas called him and handed him the phone. "It's the duty officer." he said.

Amery took the phone, and nodded a 'thankyou' to Thomas.

"DI Amery here!" he started "I understand you had a sighting for Thomas Cooper last night, and I want to know the current situation."

"Yes, sir. One of our PCs caught sight of him and followed him to an address in The Loke. He reported it immediately and we have got the house under surveillance, Sir. CID have been informed, and I can transfer you to them, if you just hang on a second." The phone went dead for a couple of minutes.

Amery thought, "Thank God there's none of that lift music!"

Then someone spoke, "DI Amery? I'm DS Hepworth. We have got your man under surveillance. He's at a house in The Loke in East Dereham. HQ have been informed, we've got a warrant and we're ready when you give us the go ahead to go in."

"That is really good news. I believe the house belongs to a James Turner. It was in Cooper's address book, but I don't want to lose him, so can you get a move on and get him asap?" replied Amery.

"No problem. I'll let you know when we've got him, and you can come and collect him!" DS Hepworth replied.

"Thanks. Let me know when you're going in, and any info you get on this James Turner. I don't know how he is connected, so you better take him too."

"Will do." and DS Hepworth ended the call.

Amery turned to Thomas "Now we wait!" and Thomas nodded, just as Merriweather entered the unit.

"Good morning! I picked up doughnuts for us."

He handed the box of doughnuts to Thomas as he removed his jacket and hung it up.

"Thought we might be hungry!" he continued, glancing over to Amery, who showed no visible signs of knowing what he was talking about, but he said,

"We've got some good news, Merry. Cooper has been seen and hopefully they will capture him today. Another trip for us! We will need to go and pick him up. Pete, I may need you to come too." he said, looking across to Thomas who nodded.

It was now eight thirty am, and Corinna entered the unit, "Sorry I'm late, I stopped off to pick up doughnuts!" she said and looked across the room and saw the bag of doughnuts near the kettle. "Oh dear! And I thought it was a good idea at the time!"

Amery smiled at her, that mischievous twinkle in his eye putting her at ease, and said, "Never enough doughnuts for a busy office like ours! Now, is someone going to make that coffee, so that we can have one?"

Johnson arrived a few minutes after Corinna, just in time to enjoy coffee and doughnuts. Everyone in the unit was in good spirits. Amery, in particular, was pleased with the progress. But he felt a little apprehensive, waiting for the call from Norfolk. Within minutes of his thoughts he got a call from Norfolk.

"DS Hepworth here, just wanted you to know we are going in at ten am. HQ are sending over some extra bodies, so I'll call you again when we get him and the James Turner whose house it is." Amery thanked him, and the phone went dead.

"OK, the good news!" he spoke aloud to everyone in the unit "They are going in at ten am. The bad news?" Everyone in the room held their breath, waiting for him to continue "We have almost two hours to wait." and he smiled at them.

Everyone in the room laughed a little, then continued with their tasks. Merriweather and Johnson were still going through photographs and matching them to any young women. Thomas continued to collate the information he had from Merriweather and Amery, together with the copies of the statements, and Amery and

Meriweather's pocketbooks, and Amery's notebook from the Plymouth trip. He added the salient information to the board. Corinna was still typing up from the tape that Amery had given her. She stopped every now and again, removed her earphones and took deep breaths, as the information she was taking in hit her. Thomas noticed, and went over and quietly spoke to her,

"Are you OK?" and she whispered to him,

"He's a bloody bastard, Peter." then put her earphones back in her ears and continued typing.

Thomas gently placed his hand on her shoulder, tapping it twice, before going back to the board, continuing what he was doing, but keeping an eye on her.

Johnson turned to Merriweather saying, "I think I've found another connection!"

He showed a photograph of a young woman leaning against green double doors, of what looked like a Victorian stone building. Then he showed him another photograph which showed the same green doors on the corner of large red brick building. There was a name over the doors, but it was difficult to read.

Merriweather took a magnifying glass and tried to read the sign, but it was still too blurry, so he said, "Right, we'll put those two together over here." - placing them on a separate place on the table - "Keep them together, and see if anyone here can figure out where they were taken. Meantime we can continue to look for more. By the way, Johnson, have you spoken to any of the young women

212

whose photographs were in the loft at Coopers?"

"I spoke to three of them, but they had no idea that anyone had taken their picture. I asked them if they had known Sofia, and they all said that they had known her, and were friends, but not close friends. I asked them if they knew Cooper, and they all said they didn't know him, but knew of him. They had seen him with his collie sometimes walking around town, and had even spoken to him and stroked his dog, but that was as far as any 'relationship' went."

"There were two other photographs of girls, but I don't know who they are, but I've spoken to my sergeant, who was going to show it to the other beat officers, and get them to keep an eye out for them."

"Having seen the photographs, I think they were taken with a telescopic lens. I have written it all down in my pocketbook and asked Corinna to type it up for you."

Amery had been listening to their conversation and said, "Well done, Johnson! Now, can you pass the photographs you found over here, and let me see if I might recognise where they were taken?"

Merriweather picked up the two pictures and passed them to Johnson, who took them over to Amery, then returned to the mound of pictures that still remained on the table. Amery studied the photograph, but he didn't recognise where it had been taken. He took them across to Thomas to have a look. He too had no idea where they had been taken and, almost in desperation, he took them to Corinna, interrupting her with a tap on her shoulder.

She took the earphones out and turned to Amery,

"I think I'm nearing the end, sir." she said.

"No, it's not that Corinna, I just want you to have a look at these photographs and see if you can tell me where they were taken, like we have been doing with the photographs."

She took the photographs from his hand, and almost immediately said, "That's Salford Lads Club!"

Amery opened his large green eyes in amazement. "How can you be so positive?" he asked her.

"Because The Smiths recorded "The Queen is Dead" and that picture is on the cover of their album. They are standing outside of those green doors. It's very distinctive and I reckon, from the clothes that lass is wearing, it was taken some time in the nineteen eighties.

"Well, thank you Corinna! You are amazing!" he said to her.

She popped the earphones back in and continued typing with a broad grin across her face, which slowly faded as she listened to the recording.

"So!" said Amery to Thomas, "Salford, I believe, is Manchester, so you better give them a call and see what you can find out. You can say we think it's around the nineteen eighties, and see if they have any unsolved cases there."

"Right, guv, I'll do that immediately!"

He picked up the phone and called HQ to get a direct number for Manchester CID. Within half an hour he had made the call and faxed the photograph through, together with the two photographs of Cooper, though they should already have had them, and thought to himself, "Now we wait!"

At eleven thirty am the telephone rang, and all eyes turned to Thomas, who answered the call.

"Hello?" He waited then said, "Hang on, sir, I'll pass you over to my guv'nor." He walked over and passed Amery the phone, saying, "It's Superintendent Crabshaw from Norfolk Police."

Amery put the phone to his ear. "Yes, sir, DI Amery here." and he listened intently and bit his bottom lip. His sparkling green eyes turned grey. "Thank you sir, I'll wait to hear anything further from you." and he put the phone down.

He didn't speak for a few moments, rubbing his hand across his forehead and eyes. The office was silent, and everyone had turned and looked at him, waiting to hear what he had just heard. It wasn't good news, that was for sure. Amery composed himself. He wanted to swear and curse, but didn't. Then he said, "They didn't get him!"

"Oh! Shite!" said Merriweather "What the fuck happened, guv?"

Amery replied, "Apparently as soon as the PC reported the sighting and the address he had gone to, CID were informed and dispatched for surveillance, but they think, between the sighting and them getting there, Cooper left! Of course, they didn't know that until they had received the warrant and gone in at ten am, as planned. However, they've taken James Turner in for questioning."

"At the moment, they don't think Cooper left because he was spotted, so that could be a good thing, and he may not go to ground if he doesn't think we are that close to him. But we will wait and see what this Turner has to say. The Super' was very apologetic, but it was just bad luck and once again, we wait."

Amery opened the address book again and then said, "Pete, Merry, anyone have a map?"

Thomas was first to reply, "No, guv, but I can get one!"

Johnson interrupted and said, "I have one in the car, I'll get it for you."

He hurried out through the door to his car and returned within seconds, with what appeared to be a large fold-up map. On its front was printed 'Map of the UK'. He handed it to Amery.

Amery opened the map, but it was huge. "Anywhere we can pin this up, Pete?" he said.

"I'll make a space on the wall over here, guv. I've got Sellotape." He turned to Johnson and said, "Hope you don't mind a bit of sticky tape on your map, and I hope it doesn't tear it for you, but we can't get pins into these bloody unit walls. They're all-metal!"

"Don't worry, Stuart, we can replace it for you. Pete, put an order in for a new one for him, or pick one up and take it out of petty cash."

Amery took the map over to Thomas and, between them, they got it up on the wall. Amery asked Thomas to mark the map with the locations of all the known incidents.

When Thomas had done this, he and Amery stood back and inspected them, looking for patterns or something that connected them.

Merriweather, who had been looking on, stood up and walked over. Standing next to Amery, he studied the map a little closer, then said, "Funfairs! Didn't his wife say he was an engineer and travelled, maintaining machinery at funfairs?"

"Look, guv, what we have, and there may be more, but the first one in nineteen seventy-two, you could say he got over-amorous, he was about twenty-four. Then he meets his wife at a funfair, and they move from Bristol, where he was working on a funfair, to Plymouth. I can only guess he married her because she was so different from the other young women he became involved with. Let's be honest, nice lady as she was, she was very plain and, can I say, ordinary. Anyway, he moves to Plymouth."

"His hobby was photography, so he's going out onto the moor, or near the moors, to take photographs, and sees the hitchhiker, picks her up, but fell foul and drove off. Next, we know he's in Blackpool."

"OK, funfair there, and he sexually assaults the next young woman. Now he returns home and goes out again, on or near the moors, to take photographs, and meets that lass,"- he pointed to the name Susan Ford - "and he rapes her. So, he's now gone from sexual assault to rape and it's about this time that he starts on his daughter."

"I bet you anything that the girl in that picture in Salford was also raped. There is a funfair not far from Salford, I guarantee. And, I also bet he raped that lass, Brenda King, when his wife threw him out, because that's the only one in his home town, at least that we know of, not counting his daughter of course, before he moves this way and sets up here."

Amery smiled. "You think the same way as me, Merry! But this means that there might have been more and there probably will be more. He is a serial predator, and he went from assault to rape to murder. He was planning more definitely, I guarantee it, and that's why he had those photographs in his loft. Whether he wanted to rape them or murder them we don't know, but we have got to catch him, and soon!"

He opened the address book and once again flicked through the pages, looking at the addresses and the map on the wall.

"Where did he go from Dereham?"

He wasn't really asking, just pondering the question while flipping through the pages in the book.

"Unless John Turner gave him a car, or he bought one, which I doubt at this stage, he must use public transport, so where can he go from Dereham? He probably doesn't know how close we were to him, so he is more likely to make a slip. He thinks he is infallible, especially as he told us he found the body of Sofia, and must have been bloody well laughing at us!"

Amery was fuming but continued to look at the addresses in the book and look at the map.

"I don't think he would go west, it would bring him too close to us, so I reckon he must have gone south. Can't go east, it's sea!"

Then as he turned a page he said, "I've found an address in Thetford. Now how would he get from Dereham to Thetford?"

Corinna looked up and removed the earphones. "I've finished that tape, sir. I'll print it out." she said. After a few clicks on the keys, she stood up and walked across to the printer. As the sheets came out, she carefully removed them, one-at-a-time until they were all out, and then she stapled them together and passed them to Thomas, saying, "I'll get cracking on PC Johnson's pocketbook now!"

Amery smiled at her again and said, "Corinna, you are a mine of information! So how do you think I would go from Dereham in Norfolk to Thetford in Norfolk?" and he pointed at the two points on the map.

Before she returned to her chair she walked over to the map, looked at it for a while and said, "Well, if those dotted lines on that map are train lines, I would go from Dereham back to Norwich and then get a train directly to Thetford from there."

Amery, Thomas and Merriweather peered at the map again, and all three of them smiled. Amery said, "Thank you, Corinna. You should be a detective!"

She looked at him, smiled, and saw that twinkle in his green eyes had returned. Then, smiling herself, she went back to her desk, opened Johnson's pocketbook and started to type it up.

"Thomas!" said Amery "Call Superintendent Crabshaw back for me."

"Good afternoon again, sir. It's DI Amery again, I'm actually calling about a property in Thetford where we think Cooper might have gone. It is thirty percent deduction and seventy percent guesswork. We haven't heard anything yet about any information your chaps have managed to get from James Turner, and I would appreciate you holding him as long as you can, so he can't contact Cooper."

"However, in Cooper's address book we have found a Chas Fuller at, 27 Magdalen Street, Thetford IP24 2BN. I haven't done a CRO check on him as I've only just found the address, but I wonder, sir, if you could get CID down there to check it out for us? I know you will understand my hesitancy to contact the local CID myself, and I thought if you explained what happened in Dereham they might proceed with extreme caution. Of course, sir, you understand Cooper may well not be there, but it could be a possibility!"

Amery took a deep breath and waited for the response. Then after a few moments listening to the reply, he said, "Thank you very much, sir." and put the phone down. Then, turning, he said,

"Well, chaps, he is going to do that for us!"

It was now about three pm, and Corinna was once again making everyone coffee and passing round more of the doughnuts. No one had left the office all day, and while Amery didn't feel hungry, he realised that no one had eaten anything except the doughnuts. Amery was about to speak to them all when the phone rang again, and Thomas answered it.

"Yes. Yes. OK! Can you fax that information over, please, and we will keep you up to date with our enquiry too. Thank you!" He turned to Amery and said,

"We've got another match! Pauline McLeod, then sixteen years old, raped in a place called Seedly Park in Salford in nineteen eighty-nine. That is her in the photograph outside Salford Lads Club."

"Better get confirmation from the photographs that we sent that it was him, and if they can trace the girl, sorry, woman, now, and if she is willing to give evidence if we catch him? Hold that, when we catch him!" Amery said.

He turned to Corinna. "More typing for you, lass." and she responded, "No problem, sir."

Merriweather said, "I think there is a fun fair or adventure place not far from there, so it wouldn't surprise me if he has worked there.

Corinna called out, "There's a place called Gulliver's World in Warrington, and I'm sure it opened around that time. In fact, my parents took me when I was a teenager. It's like a fun fair with adventure places and rides."

"Thanks, Corinna. That fits with Cooper being an engineer. He could well have been working there." Thomas replied.

It was now nearly four thirty pm and Amery was still thinking about food for them all. He nearly said something earlier, but the phone had interrupted him so first he said to Thomas,

"Can we ensure that any calls to this unit are diverted to either my phone or yours?"

Thomas replied, "No problem, guv'nor, I can do that, but why?"

Amery said, "I think we all need to get something to eat, so dinner is on my tab. Divert the calls, pack up, and let get ready to go. Johnson, have you any casuals with you?" he asked him, as he was still dressed in his uniform, whereas the others were all in casual clothing or plain clothes.

"I haven't, I'm afraid, sir, but I don't live far away. Perhaps I could meet you, if you tell me where you are going, and I can nip home and change." he replied.

"OK, that's fine! We can go to the Wild Buck. Does everyone know where it is?" Amery asked, and everyone said they did.

"OK, let's meet at six pm. I'm just going to nip home and I'll get a cab back, so if anyone wants to do the same it might be a good idea!"

Amery snapped the address book shut and put it into his briefcase, closing it. Picking it up, he left the unit and got in his car. He drove home and dropped his briefcase in the hall. He didn't change. He just telephoned a cab company to pick him up in thirty minutes; enough time to give Julia a quick call. He dialled her number and she answered immediately.

"Hello! Nice to hear from you, Simon." she said.

"Hello Julia, how are you? he asked her.

"OK, thanks, it's been another busy day at the mall. Couple of shoplifters, and a scuffle with some youths, but I'm sure not as pressurised as your day!" she replied. Then continuing in a soft seductive voice, "So what are you doing tonight?"

"Well, that's why I'm calling, really. I can't see you tonight." He paused, as he could hear her take a breath, "but if I can, I'd like to see you tomorrow, and perhaps you could come to my place?"

Disappointed at first, but relieved that he still wanted to see her, she replied, "I would like that!"

Amery continued, "I'm taking my team out to the pub tonight. They have been working bloody hard, and it has been quite intense this last week, and when it got to about four o'clock I realised no-one had eaten, not taken a break, and had been working all day, and to top it, we had a disappointing situation with the case. Anyway, I thought I'd give them a break, and a few pints. I'm just waiting for the cab to pick me up, but wanted to hear your voice, to cheer me up."

He tried to put on a slightly pathetic voice in the last few words, saying, "I can't promise about tomorrow night. You do understand, don't you?"

"Of course I do, Simon. It's nice to hear your voice too, and know you are thinking about me, as I you; and I do understand. What's the expression? 'A policeman's lot is not a happy one'!" She waited for him to reply.

"Oh! Gilbert and Sullivan fan, then?" he laughed.

"Not really," she started "but anyway, I hope I do see you tomorrow, but I really do understand if you can't make it, and appreciate you calling. Have a good evening and relax, and don't drink too much!"

"I'll try!" he said "Good night!" and he put the phone down.

His cab arrived by five fifteen and took him to the pub. Merriweather, Corinna and Thomas were already there, and Johnson arrived twenty minutes after him.

He put a tab up behind the bar, and ordered more rounds of drinks for everyone, giving them menus to put their orders in. They ate, drank, and got pretty rowdy, though Amery was careful to keep his wits about him. He didn't receive any diverted calls, and a part of him was glad, because it gave him time to relax with his team.

He turned to Johnson, whom he hadn't really noticed before in much detail. He had only seen him in uniform, and all policemen look different when they are in civilian clothes. He was smart, he hadn't turned up in a pair of jeans, but had taken the trouble to put on a pair of grey trousers, and a white shirt and tie and, he noticed, he had very clean shoes. "This is a chap that cares about his appearance." he thought to himself, before speaking to him. "Johnson, when you come in tomorrow don't wear your uniform, just come in civvies and don't worry, I'll clear it with your boss!"

"Thank you, sir." he replied "Can I get the next round?" he asked everyone.

Merriweather replied, "And why not?"

And so the evening continued, everyone getting very merry and happy until closing time, when they were all asked to leave.

Amery got them to call a cab for himself, offering to give anyone a lift, but Merriweather and Thomas decided to leave their cars and get their own cabs back. Corrina, who hadn't drunk very much, offered Johnson a lift home.

"Let's make it a nine am. start guys!" were Amery's parting words as he got into his cab.

CHAPTER 16

DAY 10

As usual Thomas was first to arrive, Merriweather followed about five minutes later, then Johnson followed in less than five minutes after that. It was now only eight fifty-five. Amery arrived dead on nine oclock, and Corinna came in, doughnuts in hand at nine ten and, as she walked in, said in a very cheery voice,

"I hope no one got doughnuts this morning except me! I'll make the coffee, and sorry I'm a bit late, sir."

She proceeded to make coffee for everyone, handing out the doughnuts. Amery just smiled at her. He didn't have a hangover, or a sore head, or headache, but looking at Johnson, thought he might.

Amery put in a call to Johnson's boss and thanked him for allowing Johnson to help. He told him he was an asset to the case, and much needed, and just to let him know he was working in his civvies. His boss said it was

OK, and he could stay with them as long as needed.

"All cleared with the boss!" Amery said to Johnson, continuing, "Nice to have you onboard!"

"Thank you, sir." said Johnson.

Merriweather joked, "You can just call him Guv. We all do!"

Johnson nodded.

Thomas took the diversion off Amery's phone, just as the office phone rang.

"DC Thomas, how can I help you?" he said, as he picked the phone up and listened to the reply. "Just a moment, Sir, I'll pass you over to DI Amery." and in doing so said "It's Superintendent Crabshaw from Norfolk."

"Good morning, Sir, good news for me, I hope?" Amery wasn't a religious man, but he was praying for good news.

At the other end of the line, Crabshaw told Amery that indeed, Cooper was in Thetford, and that he had wasted no time in drawing a warrant and picking him up. It had all happened the night before, but it was past midnight when they went in, so he waited until this morning to let him know, and when did he want to come and collect him? They had also picked up Charles Fuller, with whom he was staying, and although they were not going to question Cooper, they would start questioning Fuller. Crabshaw was aware of the case, and he realised it was pretty complex. He said they could hold Cooper for twenty-four hours without charge, and this could and would be extended on his say-so, if necessary.

Amery was delighted and thanked Crabshaw. He said he would make the necessary arrangements and, if at all possible, would pick him up later that afternoon. As soon as he put the phone down, he gave a triumphant grit of his teeth and clutch of his fist.

"Gotta make arrangements to pick him up! I'll take Merriweather and you, Johnson." he said, turning to Johnson who replied

"Thank you, guv! It will give me great pleasure to be there."

Johnson thought the sight of him might just unsteady Cooper. After all, it was Johnson who had first met Cooper at the scene, and had been compassionate to this elderly gentleman, who had just discovered the body of a poor young woman!

"Peter, make the arrangements with HQ, and please ask them to make sure every bit of paperwork is checked and double-checked. I can't afford to make any mistakes. See if you can get me a car from the pool, then put a call into Plymouth to DI Graham."

Amery was pleased to tell DI Graham that they had collared him, so when Thomas passed the phone, Amery said,

"Hello, John! Great news! Cooper has been caught and arrested! He's in Norfolk, but I'm going to collect him and bring him to back to our patch. Probably start the interview tonight. Can you go and see Marilyn and Gloria Cooper? You know on the QT to make sure Gloria is willing to give evidence, and perhaps she has now told her mother. Take Caroline with you. I also need you to confirm that Brenda King will give evidence, and can you make arrangements to take formal statements from them and confirm that they are willing to appear in court?"

"No problem, and I'm glad you've got him. Now your job begins!" replied Graham. laughing.

"I know!" Amery said "So let's get him tied up tight, and I look forward to visiting Plymouth under more pleasant circumstances. We'll keep in touch!" and he put the phone down.

Within the hour the call came back from HQ, and it was all arranged. Thomas said he would drive them to HQ, and they could pick up the relevant documents, and the car. Merriweather drove the brand-new Ford Mondeo. Amery sat in the front passenger seat and Johnson sat at the back. They had telephoned Superintendent Crabshaw, and Thetford Police Station were expecting them to arrive around two pm.

Amery was in good spirits but during the journey had realised he hadn't telephoned Julia to tell her their date was off, so he suggested they stopped for a rest break.

Merriweather said the journey was probably less than two hours, but Amery insisted, and Merriweather pulled in very near Thetford, at a roadside mobile café near a public toilet. Amery went straight to the gents, while Merriweather bought three cups of coffee from the café.

Amery telephoned Julia from the public toilet, thinking, "I can't believe I'm doing this!" and laughed to himself.

"Julie!" he said as she answered "I'm really sorry I have to call tonight off. I'm actually on my way to Norfolk to pick up a prisoner. A big break in the case, so I'm really sorry..." then he stopped talking for a moment to let her reply.

"It's OK, Simon. I appreciate, as I said, that a policeman's lot is not a happy one!" and she laughed. "I really do understand, so call me when you can. Keep safe!" And she ended the call.

Amery felt a wave of emotion come over him. She was so understanding, so undemanding, so beautiful ,and he thought was this love again, and not just lust?

There was a knocking, or pounding, on the door, and a voice shouting. "You still there, guv? I've got you a coffee here!"

Amery called out, "Be there in a minute Merry a bit busy at the moment." He left the conclusion of that statement to him!

When he returned to the car, the three of them drank their coffee and having stretched their legs, disposed of the cups and continued on to Thetford.

Thetford Police Station was on the main road and really easy to find. They parked the car in the police station yard, at the rear, and the three of them walked around to the front and into the police station. Amery walked up to the desk first and spoke to the sergeant on duty.

"I'm DI Amery from Cambridgeshire Constabulary. Here to pick up a prisoner." He produced his warrant card and presented it to the officer on the desk. "This is DS Merriweather," and Merry showed his, "and this is Constable Johnson." and he took out his warrant card and waved it at the officer on the desk.

"We've been expecting you, sir," replied the sergeant. "Come in through that door."

He pointed to a locked door to the left of the desk. The door buzzed, and the three of them walked through. Once inside, the sergeant took them to the canteen and offered them coffee, which he prepared and gave to them while they waited.

"Won't be long sir! Hope you don't mind waiting, the Super wants to have a word with you, and I'll call him now that you have arrived. He can be here in fifteen minutes."

Amery responded, "Thanks, Sarge. We don't mind waiting. How's our prisoner?"

The sergeant replied "Comfortable! Do you want to see him?" but Amery declined and said he would wait.

The sergeant left them in the canteen, and they sat at a table drinking their coffee while uniformed officers entered, had coffee or tea, and then left. A couple of constables stayed in the canteen, drinking and eating sandwiches they had purchased from the automat. After fifteen minutes the door to the canteen opened, and in walked the chubby looking, smartly dressed, fresh faced Superintendent Crabshaw. The constables sitting at the table immediately stood up, as did Amery, Merriweather and Johnson.

"Sit down, gentlemen." said Superintendent Crabshaw, and waved his hands, motioning all to sit. "I'll join you for a coffee!" he said, looking around the canteen, and one of the constables at a table immediately got up and said "Milk and sugar, sir?"

He replied, "Thank you, lovely!" and sat down with Amery.

"So," Crabshaw started "tell me about this villain!"

Amery looked across at him, and around the room, and spoke in a low voice so as not to be overheard then leaned slightly forward toward the superintendent;

"I'm not sure how much you already know, sir, but he is wanted primarily in connection with the murder of a young woman on our patch. However, since the investigation started, we have linked him to several sexual assaults and rapes. My fear is there are more. He slipped through our fingers initially because we got side-tracked. My own fault, can't blame anyone else, but he is a sneaky bastard. He returned to the scene of the crime and supposedly discovered the body. As far as we can tell, he has never before returned to the scene of any of his crimes, but this was his first mistake, although at that particular time we didn't realise it. Once we connected him, it was too late to catch him, as he had already done a bunk.

On searching his premises, we have connected him to several other incidents, as I said. I have to tell you that he molested and raped his own daughter, and started on her when she was a young child so, in effect, he is also a paedophile. We have yet to connected him to any other cases of this sort, but he appears to like young and under-age women, as opposed to children, but the case is still open on that. I think it might be helpful if your guys interviewed his associates, although it would appear he carried out these crimes on his own. They may be connected in some way, or have the same penchant as him. I want to thank you, sir, for all your help in catching him. PC Johnson here is the only one who has actually seen him." Amery sat back.

"Well, good job done here!" said Crabshaw "Now when you have finished your coffee, let's get this prisoner of yours. I'll authorise the extra time you need to hold him, so you can get him back to your patch. He's been fed and watered, so you can get him to interview as soon as you like!" he said as he stood up.

Amery, Merriweather and Johnson did the same, and followed him to the holding cells, where the officer on duty opened the door. Crabshaw stood to one side and

Amery walked in, followed by Merriweather. The cell was small, and Johnson was half in and half out of the cell, but had his handcuffs ready. His eyes flashed with anger as he glowered at Cooper.

Cooper was seated on a metal bed with a thin mattress on top. There was a stainless steel lavatory in the corner of the cell with a low stainless steel wall to one side of it.

Amery and Merriweather walked into the cell. Cooper stood up and backed up against the wall. He was as Johnson had described him, and as they had seen from the photographs. He was in his early fifties, around five feet ten inches tall, with short dark hair, though there was no greying at the sides. It looked like he had dyed that part of his hair. Although fairly tall, he looked somewhat pathetic, with a greying pallor.

Amery approached him, "Thomas Cooper, I am arresting you in connection with the murder of Sofia Archer. You do not have to say anything, but it may harm your defence if you do not mention, when questioned, something which you later rely on in court. Anything you do say may be given in evidence. Do you understand?" Cooper nodded.

Amery said firmly, "Speak up, man!" and Cooper mumbled, "Yes."

Amery put his right hand out towards the cell door, while keeping his eyes fixed firmly on Cooper. Johnson handed his handcuffs to Merriweather, who passed them to Amery, who put them onto Cooper's wrists, securing his hands behind his back. Cooper glanced over at Johnson, who was staring at him, and then averted his eyes and looked towards the floor.

Johnson's mind was running wild with thoughts of wanting to fly across the cell and beat the life out of Cooper, but he kept calm. He had never been in this sort of situation before. His policing had involved minor crimes, shoplifting and traffic incidents, and he had never felt such a fool as he did now. How could he have let this bastard slip through his fingers? He blamed himself for not noticing something, though he knew he had followed all the police procedures to the letter, and anyway how could he have known?

Amery said to Cooper, "We are taking you back to Peterborough, where you will be interviewed. You have the right to consult a solicitor, should you wish to do so, and I will advise you again of these rights once we are ready to interview at Peterborough. Do you understand?"

Cooper again nodded but this time replied, "Yes." in a subdued voice.

Taking Cooper by the arm, he escorted him out of the cell. Johnson moved aside and Merriweather walked in front of them. Amery thanked the superintendent with a nod as he passed, and they proceeded to the back of the police station, where Amery carefully unlocked the handcuffs on Cooper and, keeping one cuff on his left wrist, put the other cuff on his own right wrist, before walking out of the police station toward the car. Merriweather unlocked the car with the remote and told Johnson to get into the back passenger seat. He then instructed that Amery would put Cooper in the middle, and with this in mind, Johnson should put Cooper's right wrist in the handcuffs he handed him, and put his own left wrist in the other cuff. Cooper would be secure. Cooper never said a word, just complied with any instructions he was given.

Thankfully the car was a fairly spacious saloon, and there was ample room for the three of them in the back seat. Ensuring that Cooper had a safety belt on him, both Amery and Johnson buckled up in the back of the car.

Amery spoke to Merriweather when they were all set to go, saying, "Let's get out of Thetford, then put the blues and twos on, to get back asap, and then we'll go to HQ for interview."

Merriweather replied, "Right, guv!"

And they did. Not stopping on their way back, they made it back to headquarters in less than an hour. Cooper did not utter one word. He just held his head down, looking neither to the left nor the right.

It was five thirty pm when they arrived at HQ.

Merriweather drove them directly into the police station yard, and parked up. Johnson undid his handcuff and took them off Cooper. Amery handcuffed Coopers hands together behind his back once again. Taking him inside with Merriweather, they went immediately to the custody suite, where he was booked in.

Amery said to the custody sergeant, "Keep him until the morning. Feed him and water him. I'm going to see the super, and be back first thing to interview him. He's been mirandized." He handed him over to the sergeant.

Merriweather didn't need telling what to do next. He returned the keys to the car that they had used, then he took Johnson to the canteen, to wait for further instructions while Amery went to the superintendent's office. Amery knocked on the door, opened it, and walked in without waiting for a reply.

"Good afternoon, sir," he started. The superintendent looked up at him and, before Amery continued, "I received a call from Superintendent Crabshaw. Well done, District Inspector!"

"Where are we now?" he asked.

"I've got him booked in, sir, and he's been given his rights. Superintendent Crabshaw gave me the extra time, as we travelled to Thetford to get him and bring him back. I've told the custody sergeant to feed him, water him, and let him sleep, and I'll interview him tomorrow. He was picked up at approximately eleven am this morning, and I didn't want any mistakes. It might be held against us if we started the interview tonight."

"We have a lot of evidence which is held at the unit over in Newpark, and the team over there are still working on more stuff that we have gathered."

"I'd like to interview him over here, sir. I think it

would be better than in Newpark. I don't want to tell the parents of the dead girl yet, or not until we formally charge him with her murder. There is a list of rapes and sexual assaults going back several years as well, and we have victims who are willing to formally identify him and give evidence."

"If we start the interview tomorrow," he paused, and sarcastically said "after his breakfast, we have another twelve hours before applying for further time, or we can charge him with the murder or one of the other crimes. Is that OK with you, sir?"

"Very good, Amery!" he responded, continuing "I feel sure we can give you the extra time, if needed, before formal charge."

"This is a murder, and therefore we can utilise the extra time. I'll make sure the Chief Constable is aware. Have a good night's sleep, and well done to you and your team!"

Amery thanked him and left his office. He walked a little taller on his way to the canteen but before going in he took his phone from his pocket and called Julia. When she answered he spoke immediately,

"Really sorry, but this is a quick call. I'm over in Peterborough, but should be heading home soon, via Newpark, to pick up my car. I will get home about seven thirty. Do you still want to come over, and I'll order a take-away for tonight? I've got an early start in the morning, but you are welcome to stay as long as you like!"

It wasn't quite a question, but he hoped she understood that he was inviting her to stay for the night.

Julia was smiling, though he couldn't see her grin, she was happy he had called her and said, "I need your address!"

"Oh! Julia, I'm sorry, it's 271 Canning Place, Thorney. Are you working tomorrow?" he asked.

"I've got a late start, so I'll bring a change of clothes, if that's OK with you?"

"Of course, it is. I'll be as quick as I can, and we can order something when I get there. I'll pick up some wine on my way home. What do you fancy?" he asked.

"Whatever turns you on!" she said, and laughed a little.

He smiled, and said, "I'll see you later!" Then he ended the call and walked into the canteen.

Merriweather and Johnson looked up as he entered, and Amery said, "OK, let's go!"

Merriweather and Johnson followed him, as he turned, walked out of the police station, and got into Merriweather's car. Once in the car Amery said, "Merry, stop at an off-licence for me, before we get back to the unit."

"OK, guv." said Merriweather.

Amery, who was sitting in the front passenger

seat, turned to Johnson in the rear and said,

"Well now, Stuart, how are you enjoying being with the CID?"

Johnson was taken aback a little, as he had not expected Amery to speak directly to him but replied,

"I am enjoying it, sir, and think I would like to apply to join."

"Good for you, Stuart. And if you do, I'll put in a good word for you. But your job isn't done with me yet. You can continue at the unit helping DC Thomas. Oh, Peter, continue to go through the photos, and see if you can get any more hits!" Amery said, turning back towards the front of the car.

Merriweather pulled up outside an off-licence, and Amery got out, returning five minutes later with two bottles of wine, a large packet of assorted nuts and large tube of Pringles.

"Bit loaded up there, guv?" Merriweather smiled at Amery, and returning the smile, Amery responded,

"Mind your own bloody business, Merry! Just drive!"

Still smiling and holding the packets in his arms, he put the wine on the floor between his feet. They arrived back at the unit. Amery unlocked his car and put the wine and packs on the back seat. Nodding to the uniformed officer standing outside, and seeing two cars still at the unit, he locked his car again and walked into the unit. Merriweather and Johnson had already entered and left the door open for him.

Corinna was busily typing, and Peter was sitting at the desk still going through the photographs. He looked up and Amery said,

"We got him, and he's at Peterborough. I'm going over tomorrow with Merry, and we will formally interview him. Have you got something for me, laying out all that info?" he pointed at the white board.

Peter stood up, went over to Amery's desk and picked up a folder, which he handed to him.

Amery took the folder and opened it. Inside were neatly-organised photocopies of papers setting out the sequence of events, as shown on the white board, and statements with dates that coincided with the various and many crimes he had committed, including the evidence they had regarding the murder of Sofia and the other rapes and assaults and the indecent assault of his own daughter.

"We also got a hit on the picture from the Salford Lads Club. That involved a sixteen-year-old girl, Pauline McLeod, and Manchester Police are trying to trace her now. I've included that in the documents. I'm still working of these photographs, guv," he continued, pointing at the photographs on the table, "but thought you would probably like that on your return." He referred to the folder.

"Great, Peter! Just what we needed! I'm leaving Johnson here with you tomorrow so he can help, and I'm sure Corinna will help too."

He looked at his watch, which showed six thirty, then said,

"It's late. Go home. Get cracking tomorrow, and if anything else turns up, Peter, you know the procedure. Merry and I will go straight to Peterborough and start the interview with Cooper. One of us will call you later in the day, but if you find anything that is confirmed, call us!"

Peter nodded.

Amery turned to Merriweather, "Merry, meet me at Peterborough at eight thirty in the morning. We have to give him time to have his breakfast!" he said sarcastically.

"Will do, guv, and you have a good evening!" he replied, knowingly.

Amery picked up his briefcase, carefully placed the folder in it, then left the unit and got in his car, placing the briefcase in the well of the front seat.

CHAPTER 17

DINNER FOR TWO

Amery arrived home just after seven pm and, dropping his briefcase in the entrance hall, put the wine in the refrigerator and the snacks on the worktop. He then rushed up the stairs and directly into the bathroom. Stripping off, he jumped into the shower and freshened himself up. He could smell the stench of Cooper on him. The murder, the rapes and assaults of so many young women turned his stomach, but the hot water helped to wash away his depressing thoughts. The fact that Julia would arrive very soon lifted his heart a little. Turning the taps off, he stepped out and grabbed a towel, which he tied around his waist. He crossed to the basin and cleaned his teeth while looking at his face in the mirror.

"Do I need a shave?" he wondered, answering himself aloud, with "No time!"

Quickly drying himself off, he picked up the clothes he'd been wearing and went into the bedroom. He hung up his jacket and put his shirt, pants and socks into the linen basket. He put on clean underpants and a clean shirt and stepped back into his trousers. "Don't need socks!" he said aloud to himself. He threw the towel in the linen basket and was combing his hair as the doorbell rang. He took a quick glance around the bedroom before rushing back to the bathroom and splashing on a liberal amount of aftershave. He called "I'm coming!" as he hurried downstairs to open the door.

It was a beautiful evening. As he opened the door the sun glinted behind her, casting her silhouette in pure gold. Her long red hair flowed over shoulders, flickering in the warm evening breeze.

"May I come in?" she asked, and he realised he was just staring at her.

She seemed to get more lovely each time he saw her, he realised. Her voice awoke him pleasantly from his virtual trance.

"I'm sorry, let me take your bag!" he said, holding out his hand and taking her bag. He moved aside for her to enter. "Go on through!" he said.

She took a few more steps and the room opened up. She walked on into the lounge.

"Nice place!" she remarked as she looked around, turning back to him. "Thank you for inviting me!"

He placed her case at the foot of the stairs and crossed toward her.

"Let me take your jacket." he said to her. He gently placed his hands on her shoulders, and she slipped out of it.

She wore a short green jacket which, when removed, revealed a beautiful green dress that had one shoulder strap twisted at the front, near her waist, with a ruffle, and slit round her knees and calf. As he removed her jacket, he noticed the dress had a low back and a zip that ended below her bottom, and thought,

"What a beautiful bottom and lovely legs!" but didn't say that aloud. He kissed her shoulder and said,

"Please make yourself at home, and sit down. I'll get you a glass of wine!"

"That would be lovely!" she replied.

She sat on the sofa while he went across to the kitchen and opened the refrigerator. Taking a bottle of wine and two glasses from the cupboard, he opened the bottle and filled them. He then took them over to her, handing her one of the glasses. He placed the other on the table before returning to the kitchen. Opening the nuts and Pringles, he emptied some of them into bowls and returned to the lounge, where he put them on the table.

"I'm sorry I'm not too organised. Only got back a while ago." Then he picked up his glass and looked into her eyes saying "To a good evening!" Before he sat down, he continued "What would you like me to order? Do you fancy Chinese again, or pizza, Indian, Italian?"

"I do like Italian but, to be honest, I think a little

Chinese would be lovely. Where did you get it when you brought it over to my place?" she asked him.

He went over to the kitchen worktop drawer and took out the Chinese take-away menu and said, "From here, 'Chop Sun'. I can order again, and they will deliver here." he said.

He walked back and sat next to her, showing her the menu, which she went to take from his hand. But he held onto hers and as she looked up at him he gently touched her face, pushed her hair back and lent towards her, dropping the menu and putting his other hand around her. Pulling her to him, he kissed her gently on the lips, long and lasting, before he gently pulled away, saying,

"So, what do you want to eat?"

She smiled, then picked up the menu and started looking.

"Well, I am a little hungry, but if you will share, I'd like some Chow Mein, and I know they're messy, but I really fancy spare ribs!" she said, passing the menu back to him.

"That sounds good. And how about some sweet and sour balls with some special fried rice. What we can't eat now, we may feel hungry and want later!"

His green eyes twinkled He smiled at her and she smiled back in acknowledgement.

He got up and picking up the phone, he ordered. They told him thirty minutes, so while they waited, he

247

readied plates and cutlery, placing them on the table. He refilled the wine glasses and put the half-empty bottle in an ice bucket, and put that on the table too. He opened a drawer in the kitchen and took out some linen napkins, but hesitated taking a moment to reminisce while holding them in his hand. They had been a wedding gift. Charlotte had loved to use them as often as possible. Every time they sat down at the table to eat together, she had used them. He took them over to the table and placed them next to the plates. Julia noticed them, rose, and walked across to the table. Picking one up she said,

"These are beautiful! Do you really want to use them with spare ribs? We could use paper for now!"

"It's OK. They are better used, rather than sitting in the drawer. They do wash up OK." He was really pleased that she too appreciated the beauty in a linen napkin.

She still held them in her hands, and he noticed her skin was almost white, not unlike the pure linen napkin she held in her hand. Her skin was soft. She had long fingers and beautifully manicured and polished red nails. He held his breath for a moment, moved closer to her and taking the napkin from her hand, placed it back on the table, but pulled her close to him and again he kissed her. This time he slipped his tongue into her mouth and gently moved it around. He pulled her closer and closer, until he could feel her heart beating on his chest, and he moved his hand around her back, feeling the bare skin on her shoulders. He caressed her, and she responded by playing with his tongue with hers and running her fingers through his hair. He could have taken her there and then, and made passionate love to her on the lounge floor, but he wanted it to last and enjoy every moment, so he gently pulled away and looked into her eyes and smiled.

She smiled back and he said, "Chinese will be here soon!" and she laughed, picked up her wine glass and returned to the sofa and sat down, still smiling.

He straightened the napkins on the table and felt himself trying to look busy, while really wanting to forget the Chinese and just eat her. He paused, looked across at her then walked over to the sofa and, picking his glass up, took a sip and said to her,

"So Julia, tell me about your day."

"It was just another day," she said "a couple of shop lifters and noisy kids. A coach party came in about eleven am. I think it was an old folks' outing. No idea where they came from, but they shopped and ate and left about four pm. It's good for the shops as they tend to spend money. Thankfully the pickpockets weren't around today." She looked at him, sipping her wine again, then went on "We know who they are, so the guys let me know straight away if they spot them on the monitors, and we alert the shops, and one of the guys goes down and asks them to leave the mall. But thankfully, today they weren't in. So, what about you?" she asked him "What have you been up to?"

"Well, we took a ride to Norfolk and brought back a prisoner, who we will interview tomorrow." he started; but the doorbell rang and interrupted him. "Must be the Chinese delivery" he said, and continued "Please sit yourself down at the table and I'll get it."

He went to the door and collected the delivery. Julia went and sat at the table. He brought in the food, opening the bags on the table and taking all the containers out.

"Shit!" he said. "Oh, sorry, I forgot the serving spoons!"

He took the empty bag and went to the kitchen. Throwing the bag in the bin, he retrieved the serving spoons and returned to the table. Julia had taken the lids off the containers and had shaken out one of the napkins and placed it onto her lap.

"This looks and smells really good!" she said.

As he sat down he replied, "So do you. So do you! Here!" he said, passing her a serving spoon, and placing the others in the containers. "Do you think a bowl of water for our fingers might be a good idea?" he asked her, and she replied in a provocative voice,

"If you want, but I'm happy to lick my fingers clean. At least to begin with!" She looked at him and grinned.

"Help yourself!" he said, and they began to eat.

She left the ribs until last, and so did he. Then she picked one up and, looking at him, held the rib in both hands and running her tongue along her lips brought the rib close to her mouth and gently took a nibble at it's soft flesh, covered in a thick dark red, almost brown, BBQ sauce, that trickled down the sides of her mouth which she licked with her tongue. He watched her and lifted his rib to his mouth and, like her, took a small bite of the meaty flesh and tried to lick the sauce from the corners of his mouth. He found the experience quite seductive and thought to himself that he hadn't enjoyed ribs this much in years. They didn't speak, just watched each other eat. She ran her tongue around her lips, licking the sauce, and thinking about the next few hours she would spend in his arms.

She wanted to make the first move towards him, but she waited. She waited until she could wait no longer. Placing the bone of the rib on her plate, she lent across, gently held his face in her hands and licked him. She licked until his face was clean and no sauce remained, then kissed him on the lips and lent back in her chair; he took her face in his hands and did the same to her.

Then the two of them stood up, and he picked her up in his arms, carrying her upstairs to his bedroom. She was as light as a feather. When they arrived in the room, he stood her in front of him and, holding her close to him, slid the zip on the back of her dress down. She slipped the one shoulder strap with her hand and the dress fell to the ground, revealing her naked body. He lifted her again, gently placing her on the bed, then stood up and undressed himself. She watched him undress and let his clothes drop to the floor. He slipped off his pants and stood proudly in front of her. She gasped softly and put her arms out, beckoning him to come closer to her.

He knelt on the bed, leaned down towards her, gently lifting her flowing locks from her face, and kissed her forehead. Then he kissed her beautiful nose, her cheeks, her lips, her chin, her neck, her chest, and her breasts. Taking a nipple in his mouth, he gently twirled his tongue around it then moved to the other breast. She moved her hips with excitement, throwing her head back and arching her back and running her hands through his hair. He raised his head and looked at her face before kissing her belly, flicking his tongue in her navel and kissing her all the way down to her pubic hair, flicking his tongue and kissing and kissing her. Then he moved back up, tantalizing her. Up and up he went, and kissed her on the lips passionately.

She held her arms around his neck and played with his hair through her fingers and moved her tongue around his mouth, then she took his face in her hands and gently pushed him over to her right until he lay on his back. She rolled a leg across him until she was straddling him and, sitting on his tummy, she kissed his forehead, then his eyes, one at a time, slowly; before kissing his nose. One-by-one, she kissed his cheeks and lips and chin, his neck and chest, and she licked his nipples from one to the other, tilting her head upwards so that her brown eyes were looking into his as he opened them, their green sparkling and almost smiling at her.

She moved her leg across, so that she was now by his side, while she licked his sternum, kissed his chest and, moving herself down, she continued to kiss and lick him, until she reached his erect penis. She gently took it in her hands, and kissed it and kissed it. Then, taking it in her mouth, she licked and sucked it. He put his hands on her head and played with her hair while enjoying every moment. Then he gently pulled her up towards him and their faces met, and he pulled her close to him and kissed her so passionately he wanted it to last forever. He played with her tongue in his mouth and placed his hand on her breast, gently squeezing her nipple, then leaving it and running his hand down her belly until he felt her soft pubic hair, and moving on down until he reached her clitoris and softly moved his fingers around and, slipping them onward and into her pussy, which was waiting for him, moist and inviting. She brought her knees up, jerking her hips and groaning with pleasure.

He looked at her face. Her eyes were closed. She was smiling and slowly moving her hips from side to side. He moved down the bed and found her soft pocket, waiting for him to soak his face and lick and kiss and suck, until she moaned and pulled his head back up towards her. He rolled on top of her and she opened her legs wider to welcome him and with his hand, he gently guided his penis to find the soft wet vagina waiting for him. Pushing slowly, he too moved his hips, and she received him by pushing towards him. Their hips gyrated, back and forth. Slowly at first, then faster and harder. They groaned and perspired, their bodies moved together in perfect harmony, on and on, until an explosion of pleasure overtook the two of them, and she cried out with delight and satisfaction. He rested his head on her breasts and kissed her nipples, her neck, her lips. Then he rolled off, lying next to her and, taking her hand, kissing it, and laying it on his chest, he closed his eyes to rest, and regain his strength. She kept her eyes closed. Smiling, she breathed deep breaths of pleasure and contentment and, after a few moments, took her hand from his chest, rolled towards him, and gently put her arm over him and, resting her head on his chest, sighed and whispered

"Thank you, Simon!" then closed her eyes.

They must have slept for about an hour or so before Amery opened his eyes. He had no idea of the time, or how long he had been asleep. It was still dark, and he glanced at the clock on the night table. It showed two thirty am. Their bodies were stuck together with sweat, and he could smell the sweet smell of her perfume, mingled with their perspiration. Her head was still resting on his chest, and he gently brushed her hair with his hand and softly called her name.

"Julia." He gave her a gentle nudge, stroking her face. "Julia." She opened her eyes and smiled at him.

"Good morning!" she said in one of those husky morning voices.

"No. It's not morning, darling, but I wondered if you wanted to take a shower with me?" he asked her equally softly.

She raised her head from his chest looked around the room and realised it was still dark, then looked back at him and smiled.

"Oh yes, a shower together. How wonderful!" and they slowly got out of the bed.

He took her hand and led her to the bathroom.

"I'm so glad I had a large shower installed!" he thought, as he turned the power on and the steam started to fill the room.

He pulled her close and kissed her again, then he stepped into the shower, gently taking her in with him. He held her tightly as the water pounded on his back then turned her so she could feel its power. She threw her head back, the water soaking her hair and running down her face.

"Do you have shampoo?" she asked him.

He reached for the bottle and popped the lid on it. She took it from his hand, squeezed a little into the palm of her hands, then started to rub her hands through her hair, forming bubbles. The soap suds ran down her body and over her breasts. Some dropped into the shower tray while other soap suds continued down her flat belly and legs. He watched her patiently, but the excitement aroused him, so that he pulled her closer to him and kissed her on her lips and forehead, and nibbled at her ear and she too enjoyed the moment, becoming increasingly moist. Standing on her tiptoes, she pushed herself against his throbbing penis. She reached down and took it in her still soapy hand, gently stroking it down its length with one hand to make the skin taut and sensitive. Then she wrapped her other hand around the head of his penis and slid it up and down. He bit his bottom lip with ecstasy, tilting his head back, then bringing his head forward, kissed her on the lips again, playing with her tongue. Then he lifted her, and she put her arms around his neck. He held her up, leaning her against the shower wall, holding his hands under her bottom. The warm water beat down on their bodies. He entered her, lowering her gently, then he pushed up. She felt his full length inside her, groaned then nibbled his ear, kissing his neck as he raised her up and lowered her again and again. She couldn't help but dig her nails in his shoulder. He winced and she stopped, stroking his shoulder, kissing his neck and whispering in his ear,

"Sorry, sorry, sorry!" and groaning with pleasure, she moved her hips up and down in unison with him until he exploded inside her, and she had an orgasm like no other; that went on and on.

She clung onto him tightly, never wanting to let him go, her heart beating so fast she thought her chest was going to burst open. But it slowly subsided and he lifted her off him and pressed his weight against her, pushing her against the wall. He kissed her lips, her neck, and her breasts, then looked into her eyes and whispered,

"You are a beautiful woman, Julia!"

She smiled at him and whispered, "You are a wonderful lover, Simon!"

He took a sponge and squeezed soap on it and rubbed the soapy sponge over her body, washing her everywhere and she wiggled and moaned with delight. Then she took the sponge from his hand, squeezed more soap on it and wiped his body all over until she came to his penis. She dropped the sponge and, taking his penis between her open palms and using her hands like ping-pong paddles, very lightly batted it back and forth, invigorating and increasing its circulation, until it rose up once again and stood proudly again in front of her. She stroked it, bent down and kissed it. All the time the warm water was pounding on their bodies. He lifted her up and carried her back into the bedroom, and placed her back on the bed. They made love again and again, until the sun rose and shone through the window.

"I really must go to work, but you can stay here as long as you like, and I hope I'll see you tonight!" he said, as he got up, re-entered the bathroom, and showered.

He shaved, and cleaned his teeth. Then he returned to the bedroom with the towel around his waist. He looked across at her. She was sleeping soundly with a contented smile about her face. He quietly crossed over to the bed, kissed her on her forehead and pulled a cover over her. Then he got dressed and crept downstairs. He made himself the usual coffee, but there was no time to clear up from the night before, and the food, the containers, the plates and the napkins were left on the table, as he picked up his briefcase and keys and left the house, closing the door very quietly behind him.

CHAPTER 18
DAY 11
THE INTERVIEW

Although he hadn't had much sleep, Amery felt wide-awake and ready for the interview. As he pulled into the rear of the police station, the clock turned to eight am, and Merriweather drove in just behind him. They both got out of their cars and walked to the back entrance of the station, Merriweather pushed the buzzer on the door, looking up at the security camera pointing down at them. After a few moments the door was opened, and Amery said,

"Good morning!" as he walked past the officer and headed for the canteen. Merriweather followed. "We've got thirty minutes before we start, Merry, so I want you to look through this!

He handed him the folder Peter had prepared.

"No mistakes today! We'll follow all protocol and procedures and I want you to make notes of anything new. If I miss anything, feel free to interrupt or interject. I'll call Peter while you're reading, and find out if Norfolk got any info from the two blokes Cooper stayed with."

He went over to the window, took out his phone and called Peter. When he answered, he told him to call Norfolk and find out what they got from Turner or Fuller. He ended the call and looked through the window.

The canteen was on the first floor of the station, and at the front of the building, so he was overlooking the main street. He watched a woman on the opposite side of the road, pushing a pram with a small child walking alongside. He watched her pushing the pram with one hand, and holding onto the small child with the other, as she crossed the side road. He turned his attention back to Cooper and walked back to the table.

Merriweather had closed the file and handed it back to Amery. "When you see the whole picture like that, you know what a bastard he is!" Merriweather said.

Amery looked at him and replied "Yes, and I don't believe he realises that we now know a lot more about him and that it isn't just the murder that we are looking at!" and then, "OK, let's go see which interview room they have for us!" They left the canteen.

It only took a couple of minutes for them to find the interview room. Merriweather made sure the tape he was given was new and sealed. He opened it and put it into the recorder. The two of them stood away from the door as it opened, and an officer brought Cooper in. He was handcuffed, with his hands in front of him. Amery directed the officer to seat him at the far side of the table.

"You may remove his handcuffs, and wait outside." Amery told the officer.

Merriweather started the recorder, saying
"Thursday sixth August nineteen ninety-eight – eight
thirty-five am, Peterborough Police Station. Interview
with Thomas Cooper, date of birth twenty-sixth March
nineteen forty-eight. Present Detective Sergeant
Merriweather."

"And Detective Inspector Amery."

"Thomas Cooper, you have already been told that
you have been arrested in connection with the murder of
Sofia Archer on Monday the twenty-seventh of July, and
that you have the right to consult privately with a solicitor
if you so wish. You do not have to say anything, but it
may harm your defence if you do not mention, when
questioned, something which you later rely on in court.
Anything you do say may be given in evidence. You have
chosen not to consult a solicitor, but I will advise you
again that it is your right to do so. Do you understand?"

Cooper looked at him and said "I understand."

"Do you have anything you want to tell me?"
Amery asked him. Cooper didn't answer.

"We know it was you!" Amery said. He waited for
Cooper to answer him, but he said nothing, his eyes
averted. Amery waited, giving Cooper time to think, then
said,

"I know what's going on, Tom! Oh, do you mind
me calling you Tom?"

"No, that's OK." Cooper spoke for the first time.

"So come on, Tom, tell me what happened!" Amery waited again, but Cooper said nothing.

"Did you mean to kill her, Tom? Or was that an accident?" Amery asked.

Cooper looked straight into his eyes, and spoke again, "I didn't mean to kill her, but she started to scream and scream, and I told her to stop and put my hand over her mouth, and she was asking for it. She shouldn't have been there. She was just asking for it, with her short skirt and wiggling her arse at me. Pretended she wanted to stroke my dog, so I let her stroke the dog, and I told her she was pretty, and she smiled at me, and said thank you, and I knew she wanted it, so I let the dog lead go and grabbed her. She struggled and screamed and I dragged her where no one could see, and I ripped her panties off and she struggled more, and started to cry, and I pinned her arms and let her have it there and then on the ground, and it was a struggle too, but she screamed again and cried and groaned, so I put my hands round her throat, and she stopped screaming and I realised she had stopped breathing, and I didn't know what to do so I got off her, and did my trousers up, and covered her with leaves, and took the dog back home, and changed my clothes.

I was worried no one would find her and she didn't deserve to stay under there, so I took the dog out again and when I saw she was still there, I called you, and that young copper came, and I told him I had found her, but I knew I shouldn't have done, that so I went home again and then I left Newpark. I knew you would catch up with me. I knew you would, but it was her fault, she was asking for it. I didn't mean to kill her, and I've never killed anyone before.

These girls wear sexy clothes, they show off their bodies and ask for it, then when you give it to them they don't want it and they struggle. They have soft bodies and young skin, and they look beautiful. I like to take photographs of them, but they want it and when you give it to them, they . . ." He went silent, staring down at the table. Amery just waited and watched him.After a couple of minutes Amery said,

"Tell me more about these girls, Tom." and waited again.

Cooper looked up at him, asking "What girls?"

Amery said, "You just told me these girls are asking for it, Tom. Tell me more about them."

"They wear these sexy clothes and smile at you. You know what I mean.!" He paused, then said "Don't you know what I mean?"

Amery didn't reply. He looked at him and waited. Cooper went on,

"They like you to take their photograph. They like to pose and preen themselves like rare birds and show you their private parts like wild dogs on heat! They want you to take their photograph and they pose and make themselves provocative, and they ask for it. They all do it. They get men aroused by their behaviour and their bodies . . ."

He paused a little. He was now speaking as though he wasn't in the same room as Amery and Merriweather. After a short break he went on,

"They have such young pert bodies, and their skin is so soft and inviting!"

He stopped talking again, looking blankly across at Amery, who waited briefly, then said,

"So, Tom. Tell me when you first thought this way, about these young women?" Amery tried to sound empathetic.

Cooper stared at Amery blankly, then said, "I've always known about women, you know? Ever since I was young. I have always loved photography, and I love photographing beautiful things. I like monuments, and beautiful buildings and carvings, and beautiful things. You know I've always liked photography, and I got a camera as soon as I could afford one."

"I was an apprentice engineer, you know, and I only earned thirty-five pounds a week and gave my mother twenty-five, but I saved and bought myself a camera, and I've always loved photography." he rambled on.

Merriweather interjected, "And when did you start taking photographs of young women, Tom?" he asked.

Cooper looked at him vacuously, then looked away saying,

"Like my mother was always wanting to know everything. Always wanted to interfere with what I was doing. But some women are beautiful you know? That is, they look beautiful and are tempting. My mother was like that! She taught me about women. They are flirty and only have sex on their minds. They want to know everything about everything!" He stopped again.

Amery waited a few moments, watching him looking at the table then around the room inanely. Amery looked at Merriweather as he blinked at him.

Merriweather said "Tom!" getting his attention. "Tell me about Carol"

Cooper squinted, closing then opening his eyes. He peered at Merriweather. "Who?"

Merriweather said, "When you were in Skegness, you were working at the funfair, weren't you?" Cooper thought about this, but didn't seem to know the answer, so Merriweather went on,

"I saw a beautiful photograph of the Herbert Ingram Statue in Boston, and there was this pretty young girl standing in front of it. I think it was a long time ago, Tom. Perhaps you were only in your twenties. Do you remember?"

Cooper's eyes widened. He spoke "That was a long time ago, but I remember that girl was a tease! My mother warned me about those sorts of girls. She let me kiss her on the lips, she did, and got me all excited, then she pretended she wanted me to stop, but she showed me her frilly knickers, and let me touch her face and her private parts."

He grinned. "It was all soft and wet. I remember now, because I had never touched anyone before! Only mother."

Merriweather looked at Amery.

Cooper continued "I remember touching, and touching her, and touching her!" He was grinning.

Amery spoke "And you got married, Tom?"

He answered "Yes. But Gloria was different. She was like my mother."

"And what about Marilyn, Tom? What can you tell me about her?" Amery asked.

Cooper spoke slowly "She was my daughter." He spoke in the past tense. She was my baby! She was mine!" He was adamant, raising his voice when he said 'my' and 'mine'.

He fell silent for a bit and Amery and Merriweather waited, watching him.

Eventually he spoke again, "But she was a naughty little girl she made me . . ." He stopped again, and again Amery and Merriweather waited, but this time it was for longer, until Cooper spoke again, "She told Gloria, and Gloria blamed me!" He laughed a little then started to raise his voice again, "She blamed me! Marilyn was just like all the rest of them. They encourage you and they make you do these things. She was a very naughty little girl! So, I left and came to Newpark."

Amery waited for a bit then said, "When you lived in Plymouth, Tom; do you remember giving a young girl a lift?" and he waited but Cooper didn't react, so he continued, "She jumped out of your car and ran away, Tom. Do you remember her?" but Cooper shook his head.

Amery said, "Tom Cooper has shaken his head." then he turned to Cooper and stressed, "Tom, you need to answer me please." Cooper looked at him and said "I don't remember."

Amery looked at his watch and it was now ten forty-five am, so he said,

"Tom, I think we will have a little break now, so you can use the toilet and get a cup of tea. Give you a little time to remember things."

He turned to Merriweather and nodded. Merriweather got up, called the police officer in from outside, then returned to the recorder, saying, "Interview ended ten fifty-one." He clicked the machine off and took the tape out of the machine, sealing it.

The police officer entered the room and told Cooper to stand and put his hands in front of him. He put the handcuffs back on his wrists then led him out of the interview room. As he left, Amery said to the officer,

"Please give him a drink, and let him use the toilet, and bring Mr Cooper back in thirty minutes."

These interviews were always intense, and Amery

wondered if perhaps he needed to get Cooper psychologically assessed. This was normally the prerogative of his brief, but Cooper had refused legal representation and Amery was worried this might come back to 'bite him on the bum'. He stood up, and as he left the room he said to Merriweather,

"I'm going to see the Super, Merry. Get yourself a coffee, and a clean tape, and meet me back here in thirty minutes."

Knocking on the superintendent's door, Amery waited for him to call him to enter, then he went in and spoke,

"I'm worried about Cooper, sir. He has refused legal representation, and he is admitting all the offences he can remember, but he is strange and probably has some mental condition or something. Do you think we should get someone to look at him? I don't want to find that after all this hard work he gets off on some technicality." The superintendent looked at him and thought for a moment.

"Better get him psychoanalysed, and have the doctor take a look at him before you do any more interviewing, and I'll speak with the DPP. I'll arrange it. Take the rest of the day off and come back and see me tomorrow."

"Thanks, sir. Much appreciated!" said Amery and he left his office. Returning to Merriweather, who was back in the canteen, he said,

"Merry, go tell the custody officer to keep Cooper

comfortable. Tell him the doctor will be coming to see him, and the Super is arranging it, and that we will be back to interview him tomorrow."

Merriweather knew exactly why that was happening and just said,

"OK!"

He got up from the table, pushing a cup of coffee in Amery's direction as Amery sat down. "Thanks, Merry." Amery said.

Amery was frustrated and angry inside. He knew they had enough information and evidence to charge Cooper, plus his own admission of guilt, but he also knew that the man had serious problems. Those problems were not his concern, but if he had continued with the interview, and if they had ch had gone to trial and was found guilty, it left too many loopholes for Cooper to slip through later. If he then got representation, they might say he wasn't fairly treated and get the judgement thrown out.

This man was a serial predator of many kinds, and while he intentionally raped her, the murder of Sofia might have been an accident, though that didn't excuse him. His sentence might be reduced to manslaughter and rape, but that was for the DPP to decide, and there were too many other rapes and assaults that had to be dealt with, and the victims needed to know that he was being prosecuted for his actions.

He picked up the coffee Merriweather had passed him, and holding the cup in two hands, sipped at it. He was still thinking about Cooper, but his mind was wandering, and he found it hard to fix it on a decisive way ahead at the present time.

Merriweather returned and sat down at the table opposite him. He could see Amery was deep in thought, drinking his coffee, so he didn't speak to him. He just picked up his own coffee and started drinking it, while watching him. After a few moments Amery looked across at him, put his cup down and said,

"Merry, I think we should go and see Sofia's family, and tell them we have got him." And with that he got up from the table and, walking away, turned back to Merriweather, saying "I'll meet you back at the unit in an hour." Then he walked out of the canteen.

Merriweather mumbled to himself, with some sarcasm, "OK, guv."

He wondered if Amery had remembered they had their own cars, because if not, he would be left in Peterborough. He smiled to himself, thinking,

"He's got the weight of the world on his shoulders today!"

He knew the frustration that Amery felt, because he too felt somewhat thwarted, but he was also fully aware that it rested on Amery's shoulders, and it weighed heavily. Leaving his now cold coffee, he too left and drove over to the unit.

Amery was already there when he arrived, and he

parked up and walked in. Amery was just briefing Thomas and Johnson, telling them that he and Merriweather were going to see the family.

"Is Scott still with the family?" Amery asked Thomas.

"Yes, she's still there, guv. Said the family are planning some sort of memorial service for the kid, so that is helping them. I'll give her a call and tell her you are on your way over."

"Good!" Amery said, "I need every bit of evidence we have organised and collated, ready for the DPP. I want everything, I mean everything, sorted and ready. OK, Peter?"

"No problem, guv. We haven't found any more links with the photographs, so I'll get them put together and boxed up ready. I'll get all the forensics, and I know what to do, and I'll make sure it's done for you, guv."

Thomas could see Amery's weariness and annoyance, and understood. He also knew that the next job Amery had to do wasn't pleasant, because although he was giving them some good news about catching the person who killed their daughter, he knew they would still be unable to bury her, and closure would be a long way off for them.

Merriweather drove, and Amery was quite subdued on the drive over, but by the time they arrived outside the house, Amery had pulled himself together.

"OK, Merry, let's do this!" he said as he got out of the car.

After greeting the police constable outside the property, Merriweather knocked on the door, which was opened by WPC Scott.

"Good morning" Amery said to her, asking "Are the family together?" "Yes, sir." she said and led them into their front room, where the family were seated.

Mr Archer stood up as Amery and Merriweather entered.

"Please sit down, Mr. Archer." Amery said.

Mr Archer replied, "Will you take a seat too, and would you like a cup of tea or something?"

"We'll sit, but no tea, thank you." Amery responded, as he pulled out a chair and sat down. Merriweather did likewise.

"Well, I have some good news for you, and I am pleased to tell you that we have got the man who killed your daughter."

He waited and looked, seeing the parents of an innocent teenager. He felt so sad for them, watching as tears welled up in Mrs. Archer's eyes, but then he continued, "Unfortunately, it may be still some weeks, or even months, before you can put your child to rest."

Mrs. Archer wailed and her husband put his arms around her. She cried deeply and inconsolably. Amery said,

"I know you must be devastated, Mrs. Archer, but we all want the man that did this to be punished severely for what he did, so there isn't much more we can do now, but wait. However, I heard you were going to have a memorial service for Sofia, and I think that is a really good idea. I understand she had lots of friends who, like you, miss her terribly, and I'm sure WPC Scott here will help you in any way she can. If I can do anything for you. I will." He really meant it.

Mrs. Archer stopped sobbing now, looked up at him and said, "Thank you, Mr. Amery. I do understand, really I do, but I miss her so much. My heart aches and there is so much pain that I can't explain, and it won't go away." And she sobbed more and cuddled her husband. Amery could see the tears welling in his eyes too.

Amery stood up put his hand on her shoulder, saying, "WPC Scott will stay with you as long as you want her to, and I must tell you that once the news breaks that we have got this man, the press may try to interview you. I will make sure that there is a police officer outside twenty-four hours a day to ensure your privacy. It's up to you if you want to talk to them, but I advise against it. You have my number, or WPC Scott will contact me, if you need me."

With that he turned and left the room.

Merriweather followed. As he entered the hall he turned to WPC Scott and said, "You heard all that, so If you need me just call DC Thomas." and she said, "OK".

Merriweather and Amery left the house. On the way back to the unit, Amery told Merry to take the rest of the day off.

"Just drop me by my car and go home, Merry, you've worked too hard, and it's been a fucking terrible day!"

Amery got home at one pm. He was pleasantly surprised to see Julia's car still outside his house. Opening the door, he walked in, dropped his briefcase in the hall and checked the kitchen and lounge to see everything was clean and tidy.

She was sitting on the settee drinking a cup of coffee. He was so pleased to see her. She looked up at him, studied him, then said, "You look shattered, Simon!"

He did. He had lost the colour in his face and he felt exhausted.

"Come and sit down!" She rose, walking towards the kitchen. "I'll make you a coffee." He did as she had asked without saying a word. She made him coffee which he drank.

His first words to her, after being in the house for a good fifteen minutes were, "Why aren't you at work?" She smiled at him and said "I took a sickie! I'm the boss, so I'm allowed to."

"I'm glad you did!" he said. "You can't imagine how pleased I am to see you! It's been a shite day and to top it all I'm tired!" She knew what he meant by that, so she said,

"Well, we'll have left-over Chinese for something to eat later, and an early night."

Smiling, she sat next to him, took his head and put it on her breast.

He fell asleep.

CHAPTER 19
DAY 12

When he woke on Friday morning, he felt rested and alert. He thought about how hard his team had been working. He looked at the clock, which registered seven am. He had slept in. He was usually up by six am, but he must have been tired. Sometimes solving a major crime could take weeks, months, years, or even remain unsolved. This case had been cracked in less than two weeks. The frustration for him was that he had, as yet, been unable to charge Cooper. He hoped that today would be the day he could do it.

Julia was still sleeping. As he got out of bed he turned and kissed her forehead. She opened her eyes and looked at him. His green eyes were sparkling once again, and she smiled.

"I'll go to work later." she said as she turned over and closed her eyes again, hoping to get a few more hours of sleep.

As he washed and dressed, he felt more positive about the case, and thought to himself that he was probably over-tired yesterday, and that was what caused his frustration, yet he knew it wasn't. Anyway, today was another day.He made his coffee as usual and drank it all ,but he also remembered to wash up the cafetière and his mug before leaving.

After all she had done all the dishes from the other night so it would be unfair to leave her more dishes, he thought to himself. Picking up his briefcase and keys, he left the house, but not before listening to hear if she was stirring upstairs. But he heard nothing and closed the door quietly.

He arrived in Peterborough at eight thirty am. Merriweather wasn't there yet. He walked around to the front entrance and went into the station. The desk sergeant buzzed him into the main office. He said good morning, then went straight up to the Superintendent's office. He knocked on his door and opened it.

"Come in, Amery!" said the superintendent. "Sit down. So I bet you have been worried about this, but I can let you know it's all good news. Firstly, the doctor has said he is fit for interview, though he will need psychiatric care at some point. Between us, the doctor says that anyone who commits the crimes he has committed cannot be sane! But that's not in his report. DPP have seen your evidence, and your DC Thomas sent them a lot more stuff, and they have confirmed there is enough for them to proceed. A solicitor has been appointed for Cooper and you can have the pleasure of formally charging him this morning if you want to."

Amery felt himself sigh with relief. He said, "My

greatest pleasure, Sir!"

Amery's job was nearly done now. As he walked out of the office, Merriweather approached, and he said to him, "OK, Merry, this is it! We're charging him!"

Merriweather replied, "About bloody time!" and smirked.

It was about thirty minutes later that Cooper was brought into the interview room with his solicitor. Amery took great pleasure in saying, "Thomas Cooper, you are charged with the murder of Sofia Archer on Monday the twenty-seventh of July. You have the right to remain silent. Anything you say can and will be used…" Etc, etc, etc.

Amery's job was done. He and Merriweather went back to the unit. Thomas had almost finished boxing up the evidence and loading his car. Corinna was helping him, and the coffee mugs had long been put away. Johnson was hovering, not sure what he should be doing, but trying to look helpful.

Amery beamed at them all, saying "He's been charged! Now let's get this all cleared away, and go and celebrate!"

Then he looked at Johnson and Corinna, and said, "That includes you two!" He turned to Thomas. "Are these phones still connected?" Thomas said they were.

"Call the local station and tell them Johnson is with us for today, and he'll be back with them tomorrow, if that is his duty turn. Said Amery. "Also, tell them that WPC Scott will stay with the family as long as needed, and she will keep them up to date. Ok, Pete?"

It was two pm when they arrived at the pub. They ate and drank, and once again Amery paid the bill, before he left at five pm.

He hadn't drunk a lot himself. He stopped at an off-licence on the way home to pick up some wine. He also picked up a bottle of Lagavulin sixteen year-old Islay single malt scotch whisky, a bottle of Bacardi, and six cans of coke. He wanted to be prepared, in case Julia was still at his place. On his way home he telephoned her mobile.

She answered, "Hi Simon, sorry I missed you this morning!"

He asked her where she was, and she said at work, so he told her, "I have a couple of bottles of wine, a bottle of Bacardi and six cans of coke and a bottle of Scotch. Do you fancy coming over to my place to party tonight?

"Wow, Simon, you are going to town, so I guess everything went well?"

"Never mind that, I can tell you later, are you joining the party?" he asked.

"A party! Well, I haven't anything special to wear if I come straight from work!"

"You don't need anything special. It's only you and I!" he said.

"Then I'll be there about six thirty."

And she was...

Printed in Great Britain
by Amazon

80205236R00163